TIE ME UP

A collection of twenty erotic stories

Edited by Cathryn Cooper

Published by Accent Press Ltd – 2007
ISBN 1905170947 / 9781905170944

Printed and bound in the UK by
Creative Design and Print

Cover Design by
Red Dot Design

Contents

Skin Deep	Cathryn Cooper	1
Jane's Bonds	Shanna Germain	9
Tiger, Tiger	Paige Roberts	14
Black And White Photos	Sommer Marsden	30
My First Time	Eva Hore	40
Party Games	Jim Baker	50
Dangerous Games	Eva Hore	64
Fantasy	DMW Carol	72
Picket Fence	Sommer Marsden	78
Change Of Life	Cathryn Cooper	92
La Cage Aux Folles	Kaycie Wolfe	99
Travel Broadens The Mind	Kirsten Schubinski	111
After Hours	Kristina Wright	116
In The Saddle	Primula Bond	123
Under The Oak	Penelope Friday	135
Festival	Cyanne	143
Mistress Of All She Surveys	Carmel Lockyer	155
Teaching Derek	Primula Bond	165
Political Prey	Jim Baker	176
Maid To Misbehave	Stephen Albrow	186

Skin Deep
by Cathryn Cooper

The boy was beautiful. He'd come to stay at the insistence of a relative.

'Francis needs somewhere to stay – it'll only be for a while. Besides, it will do you good. Make you behave yourself instead of using these women the way you do.'

His aunt had been insistent. She was old and wealthy and he had no intention of upsetting her.

She was right of course; he did treat women badly. He expected and got total submission. They'd nibble his toenails if he asked them to. He was handsome, rich and never lacking for female company – physical contact only. Nothing emotional. He preferred variety for the sort of sex he enjoyed.

The boy was an encumbrance he would learn to live with. Shut him away in a room in the east wing, and that would be that. Or so he thought.

The boy, a lad of not much more than sixteen it seemed, had other ideas. Everywhere Carew went, Francis was there at his elbow.

At first it annoyed him, but over a period of weeks something happened; for a start he registered just how attractive the boy was. His hair was dark blond, soft and silky, falling over his temple in a gentle wave. His eyes were of the rarest blue and fringed with dark lashes. His lips

1

held the sensuous lines of a courtesan, full, wide and the colour of crushed rose petals.

In the beginning he had sought to escape the boy's company, but as time went on he found, much to his unease, that he sought the boy out, missing him when he wasn't around. And that smile! That soft hand easing into his, the round bottom, the hairless chin and even the scent of the lad were intoxicating.

At night he dreamed; wet dreams that he'd been inserting his cock between boyish cheeks, kissing that sweet, girlish mouth. His desires sickened but also tantalised.

His friends began to notice.

'Are you turning the *other* way?' asked one of his friends. 'It's been noticed that you're spending more time with the lad than with the ladies.'

Carew fixed him with an icy glare. 'How would you like your nose rearranged?'

The friend had laughed and pretended it was all just a joke, but Carew knew it wasn't. They had noticed his behaviour and losing face worried him. His reputation as super-stud was at risk. It embarrassed him. He had to do something about it.

Priscilla Palmer-Tovey arrived at Thompson Towers on the dot of seven. Like any parson's daughter, Prissy was polite, punctual and, although not exactly plain, she wasn't beautiful either. Carew watched her walk up the drive, straighten her hat and smooth her dress before she rang the bell. Priscilla was neat in dress but not prim when she was out of it, and at times that suited him very well indeed.

He smiled and drained the lingering dregs of whisky from his glass.

There followed a gentle knock on the door to his private sitting room which was on the first floor and had high lead-paned windows and wainscot panelling. Imran, his servant entered, bowing before making his announcement.

'Miss Priscilla Palmer-Tovey, sir.'

'As her to come up, and, Imran, tell Master Francis that I wish to see him.'

'Yes sir.'

He poured himself another drink to help drown the confusion deep in his groin. He loved women. He knew he did, so why did the boy unnerve him so much and make him think otherwise?

'Don't worry, old chap,' he muttered to himself. 'With Priscilla's assistance, it will be confirmed before the boy's very eyes. He'll not mistake your meaning, old boy. He'll get the message that you want no more of those doe eyes and come-on looks. Good God, didn't you leave all that behind you at boarding school?'

A peel of laughter preceded Priscilla's entrance. She rushed into his arms, her face flushed and hot beneath his lips.

'Darling, Roo,' she gushed, her eyes as bright as a child's on Christmas morning. 'How marvellous it is to see you again.'

She smelt of lavender and cabbage roses and her dress seemed a mixed bag of the same – pretty, floral and as busy as a cottage garden.

He smiled. 'Prissy. It's nice to see you too. I'm really glad you could come.'

Prissy's eyebrows rose. She looked surprised. 'Why, darling Roo. How kind of you. I've never heard you say that to me before.'

Now, thought Carew, I've truly spoken out of character. I never tell her it's nice to see her. Will she suspect I have a specific purpose in mind – a more urgent purpose than usual?

He smiled casually into the round face, the pale eyes and freckled nose. No, he decided, Prissy would not suspect. Like a hungry cat, she would lap up any titbit of affection he threw her and, as always, she would be malleable to his wishes.

He made an effort to control his body and make it as it always was when she appeared – rigid, unbending. All the moves were hers, all the pleasure would be his.

She ran her hands over him, her breath coming in quick, short gasps as she explored his hard chest, his tight stomach and the hot mound in his trousers. Her hand was still rolling over it when Imran returned.

Francis, eyes downcast, was right behind him. Immediately on his entering the room, something stirred beneath the hand of the parson's daughter. Carew was very aware of it. So was Priscilla. Her eyes opened very wide. With a tremendous surge of willpower, Carew reverted to polite protocol in order to disguise Francis's effect on him.

'Ah, Francis. I have someone here I would like you to meet.'

He spoke stiffly, moving his body away from the touch of Prissy's hand.

Priscilla greed Francis politely, but Carew wanted more. Grasping her shoulders he nudged her forward.

'Don't you think Francis is a good-looking young man?'

'Yes.'

'But he's shy,' said Carew, 'and you, my darling Prissy, are going to help him get over his shyness. We're going to show him something that will warm his blood. I guarantee he'll never be shy again – especially with women.'

In response to his fingers, Prissy's nipple pushed against the bodice of her dress.

Carew ordered the boy to sit and watch. Without being ordered, Imran came forward and stood beside the brown leather chair in which Carew sat down.

He smiled at Priscilla. 'Well, my dear Prissy, let us show this virgin youth exactly what a woman can do for a man, and exactly what a man can do for a woman.'

With an ecstatic expression on her face, Prissy dropped to her knees between Carew's legs and began undoing her

4

dress buttons. Generous breasts begged for release against the confining pinkness of her bra. Pushing the cups down, she brought out first one breast then the other, the nipples as big as cherries.

Priscilla's breasts disappeared between Carew's knees as she leaned forward, her hands clasping the arms of his chair. With admirable dexterity, she undid his trouser zip with her teeth.

Carew glanced at Francis. The boy was bug-eyed; no doubt he'd be playing with himself given half a chance – that is if he were inclined towards women, a fact Carew was not at all sure of.

He gave Imran the nod. As Priscilla snuffled to get his cock into her mouth, Imran's brown hands bound her wrists to the chair arms with what looked to be leather dog collars.

Priscilla was positively guzzling at his erection, licking the end, tickling the opening with the tip of her tongue.

Carew threw back his head and moaned in satisfaction. Wondering whether the boy was having an erection, he looked over at Francis and met his eyes, saw the flush of his cheeks and wondered anew…

Another nod from him and Imran lifted Priscilla's skirt, folded it around her waist and pulled down her knickers.

Priscilla squealed as Imran guided his firm, brown rod into the folded crescent of flesh poking out from beneath her thighs.

'In,' said Carew, his voice steady despite his fast breathing. 'Out,' he said.

So directed, Imran thrust and repeated on demand.

'Is she very wet?' he asked.

Imran nodded.

'She's aching for it. But you're not having it all yet, Prissy. Not until you take more of my cock into your throat. Do you understand?'

Prissy understood alright. He knew her well. Knew what she liked and what she was capable of.

5

With both hands, he manipulated Prissy's head so that her movements were suited to his pleasure. As he did so his eyes never left the face of the boy he knew as Francis.

'Now,' he said to Imran. 'Give it to her hard NOW!'

As Imran increased the speed of his thrusts, Carew pressed Priscilla's head more firmly into his lap. 'Suck! Suck me dry!'

He turned to Francis. 'Go on boy. Feel her. Press your hand between her legs and she'll come. Go on. Now!'

Francis stared round-eyed but did nothing.

Carew was furious. The moment he had withdrawn from Priscilla's mouth, he zipped up his fly leaving Imran to unbuckle the woman from the chair arms.

'Get out,' he said to both of them. 'I want to speak to Francis alone.'

'You disobeyed me. Why was that?'

The boy's cheeks were pink with embarrassment. His eyes glistened as though the shocked stare was there to stay.

'I...' he began, then swallowed. 'I didn't want to. Not with her.' And then that smile again.

With me! That's what he means! With me!

'That is that!' shouted Carew, his emotions in more disarray than his clothes. 'You've tried my patience enough. It's time you learned not to be so provocative towards me. I won't have it. Do you hear me? I won't have it!'

Francis rose slowly from the chair. 'I'm sorry. I didn't mean...'

'You didn't mean! You didn't mean!'

This was all too much. He couldn't go on feeling like this. It had to be thrashed out of the boy physically. There was no alternative, not if he was to keep his own sanity.

Before the boy could make a run for it, he grabbed his wrists, yanked him to his feet and dragged him over to the window. The curtains were held back with multi-coloured ropes; he used one of these to bind the boy's wrists

6

together. He threw the end over the overhead rail and tied it firmly in place. He tied him facing the window, anything rather than have those blue eyes beseeching him to desist.

'Please, sir…' pleaded Francis.

Carew heard him, but something about the boy's tone did not ring true. He couldn't help but get the impression that the boy was pleading for more, not to be released.

Carew clenched his jaw in anger. This confusion, he'd endured; this pain of enticement to an act unnatural to his true nature. The lad was infuriating! So he thought this would be pleasurable did he?

Smiling, he took a bundle of ornamental twigs from a tall urn and bound them together with sticky tape. The tape gave him an idea.

'Sir, are you really going to…'

Before Francis could say anything further, before the melodic voice and the big blue eyes could get under his skin, Carew placed a length of tape over the soft pink lips. He considered the eyes too, but thought better of it. It was the boy's voice that got to him.

'I'll teach you,' he said as much to himself as to the boy.

His hands trembled as he undid the boy's trousers and pulled them down. The smell of youthful flesh resurrected his flagging penis. He slapped at it, thinking it would go down. It didn't.

Fixing his gaze on the plump, round bottom, he reached for the bundle of twigs.

Concentrate. Don't look at his loins.

The twigs made a whooshing sound as they flew through the air. Francis jerked as they landed across the smooth flesh.

Carew didn't stop but raised them for a second, a third and a fourth time. Not until he'd landed six strokes did he pause to study his handiwork. What had been white flesh was now criss-crossed with pink stripes. With trembling fingers he touched what he would once have regarded as taboo territory. The flesh was so soft, so beautiful. He had a terrible urge to release his swollen member, perhaps running it between the lovely cheeks.

He groaned and closed his eyes. His worst nightmare! He desired a boy!

When he opened them again, his eyes strayed to Francis's reflection in the window. No tear escaped the clear blue eyes. The boy did not struggle but eyed him expectantly.

As though he knows I cannot resist.

He allowed his hand to touch the silken hip; he frowned. Surely it curved like a woman's?

A rush of blood blemished his cheeks as his gaze fell further down the reflection to a triangle of hair. His jaw dropped. There was no penis; not a vestige; none at all!

He ripped the tape from the full lips.

'I'm Frances, not Francis,' she said with a smile.

His jaw dropped.

'Your aunt was worried that your tastes prevented long term relationships. We hatched a plan. You see? We had a relationship before we had sex. This kind of sex. The sort I like.'

Carew finally found his voice. 'We haven't had sex.'

Her smile broadened. 'Not yet,' she said. 'But we will. We   most   definitely   will.'

Jane's Bonds
by Shanna Germain

It comes to her by mistake. Although it's her address on the plain brown envelope, it is someone else's name; perhaps the house's previous owner. She and Derek have lived here for almost five years, but they still get mail for the people that owned the house before them, people they've never met. She's about to stick the envelope back in the mailbox with a *please forward* notice on it, when something below the name catches her eye: 'Or current resident'. Oh, that's me, she thinks. It looks like junk mail of some sort, but she opens it anyway.

Inside the envelope is a purple catalogue, offering 'sexual satisfaction for women'. She lies down on the bed and starts flipping through it – she's never seen so many women-oriented sex toys in her life. Sure, she's been to Fanta-She's-R-Us downtown (once even with Derek) but it always seemed like all the products were geared toward men – videos that offered nothing more than fake boobs and way-ugly men grunting, those ridiculous-looking fake-mouths, rows and rows of cock rings.

But in this catalogue (which, she realises with little surprise, is from a female-owned company), there are tons of toys for women – cool tie-dyed dildos in pink and purple, lipstick shaped vibrators, even videos directed by women. She flips toward the back and there, tucked away on the last page, is a toy that catches her eye: two purple cuffs lined with fake fur.

She traces her hand along the page, imagining the cuffs' fur-lined softness against her skin. She's never used toys like these, but she's thought of it often, when Derek sometimes takes her hands and presses them to the bed during sex. She wonders if he'd go for it – probably not. Her husband's a wonderful man, but is still sometimes stuck in his religious upbringing, feeling guilty for anything outside of the missionary position. He's grown a lot since they met (getting him to go to Fanta-She's-R-Us was a big one) but still, he balks at things that are outside the mainstream (going to a strip club together for instance) and she never wants to push him too far or too fast. Still, she sighs, as she runs her hand over the cuffs on the page, a few toys would be nice.

She reads the description: 'Soft and delicate, yet tough in all the right ways, these fur and silk-lined bonds are sure to please.' And there's even a matching blindfold. She wonders if she should just buy them, let Derek find them somewhere in the house and act surprised. Or maybe she should put them on her wish list – her thirtieth birthday is coming up.

An image pops into her head of opening a gift like this, late at night, after a good meal and a glass of wine. Perhaps she's already opened her other gifts, and they're cuddled up in bed when Derek reaches beneath the pillow and pulls out the blindfold and cuffs. They're not gift-wrapped, but it doesn't matter because they're so soft and silky and festive already. She's about to say thank you and wrap her arms around his neck when he grins sheepishly and says, 'Shhhh…I'm afraid I'll change my mind.'

So she lies back and closes her eyes. He fits the blindfold over her eyes a little clumsily, his big fingers fumbling through her hair. She's tingling down to her toes in anticipation – it's all she can do to lay still and let him work. But she doesn't want to scare him, so she stays still, focuses on her breathing – in, out, relax – and enjoys the waves of excitement running through her body. When she opens her eyes, she can't see anything – a little aura of pink light through the fabric, but that's all.

He presses his lips to hers, and she realises she's never kissed him before without watching him lean closer and closer in anticipation of the impending kiss. But now, she doesn't know what to expect, his lips are there and then they are elsewhere, and she doesn't know how to react, how to plan. Instead, his lips light unexpected little fires wherever they land, as though he's pressing fireflies to her skin. He is kissing the curve of her neck when he whispers, 'undress for me'.

She feels a jolt of panic. Get undressed? How? She can't see anything. How will she know what she looks like? What if she does something stupid? But he is kissing her along the back of her ear, across the front of her shoulder blade, and she realises it doesn't matter, that she'll do as he asks because she wants to, because he wants her to.

He helps her to stand, and then she hears him lie back down on the bed. The room around her feels too large, too empty, too alone, even though she knows it isn't. She fights the urge to reach out for something, anything – the dresser, the edge of the bed, the closet door – and instead reaches down to find the tie of her robe. She unties it slowly, then slides it off her shoulders and lets it fall to the ground. Then, she takes a deep breath, and pulls her tank top slowly over her head and throws it over her shoulder. Her nipples are erect from the excitement and the cold air makes them pucker even more. Then she leans down, and drops her panties down over her feet, and stands back up.

She hears Derek sigh, and tries to imagine where he is in the room, what's he's doing. Then his hands are on her, trailing down her hips and across her thighs, and she realises he's sitting on the bed and she must be standing

11

right in front of him. He takes her ass in his hands and pulls her toward him, them runs his tongue across her belly button, down her thighs.

'Lie down,' he says, and it doesn't even sound like his voice. It's gruffer somehow, more forceful. 'Put your arms up,' he says, and she does, feeling his strength as he holds both her hands above her with one of his own. Then she feels him slide the cuffs around her wrists, their furry softness caressing her skin, and then tightening and pulling just enough so that she can't slide out. He hooks them to something – she's not sure what – and suddenly she can't move.

'OK?' he asks tenderly, and she can't do anything but nod. She's not sure what she feels – excitement, anticipation, fear, desire – she wants him to do whatever he wants to her. She would say yes to anything he asked.

Suddenly she realises there is silence all around her. She can't hear or feel Derek anywhere. Her skin comes alive, and she imagines this is what it's like to be in a horror movie, where you know something's coming for you, but you don't know what it is or where it's going to come from. Or like being prey – every nerve, every muscle twitching, ready to react with a flight or fight response. 'Derek?' she whispers. She's afraid to break the silence, but she feels like she has to do something. 'Derek?'

She doesn't hear anything. A pull on the cuffs only seems to draw them tighter around her wrists. Is he sitting there watching her? Did he leave her here? What if he's taping her? She knows, of course, that he would never do any of these things, but the longer she waits the more the fear creeps in.

Then, finally, she hears a noise. She pricks her ears in that direction, feeling like a wild animal. Is that him? Is it the cat? She can't tell. She feels like her senses are deceiving her. Something cold brushes against her stomach, and she has a moment of near panic – she's ready to rip the cuffs right off – but then she feels Derek's tongue too, next to the coldness, and hears him crunching something in his teeth.

He runs his tongue, along with the ice, up her stomach, leaving a tingling trail of heat and cold, until he reaches her chest and the ice melts. Her stomach does somersaults as he winds his cool tongue around one nipple and presses his palm firmly between her legs. She presses against the flat of his hand, willing him to touch her, stroke her, enter her. She has forgotten she is handcuffed to the bed that she cannot see. All of her senses are focused on just one spot – if he doesn't split her open soon she will explode.

'Please…' she whispers, 'please…'

'Please what?' Derek asks as he enters the bedroom, jolting her out of her fantasy. Her face is warm and prickly. She thinks about pretending she was asleep, then thinks better of it and hands the catalogue over to him.

'Please…please buy me these,' she says softly, pointing to the silk bonds with one tired, trembling finger.

Tiger, Tiger
by Paige Roberts

They come for me in the dead of night. Dark-skinned hands out of the dark Indian night cover my mouth so I won't cry out. There must be at least half a dozen people, all holding me. I cannot possibly fight them though at first I try. My frantically pounding heart is the only sound I hear. My wrists are securely bound with rough hemp rope, then my ankles. A wad of cloth is stuffed in my mouth and bound there with more rope that cuts hard into the corners of my mouth.

All in silence, the villagers who I dined and chatted with the previous evening carry my bound and struggling nude body above their heads out of the remote Indian village and into the deeper darkness of the surrounding jungle.

As they carry me deeper into the jungle gloom, with the sounds of night creatures and the scent of rich earth swallowing me, my panicked heart begins to slow down. I know that I am almost certain to die tonight, but I am utterly helpless to do anything about it. A resigned calm envelopes me as surely as the darkness which my eyes are slowly adjusting to. I came to this remote corner of the world seeking new experiences and adventure. Looks like I'm about to get what I came for, in spades.

A solid stone platform about seven feet by four is my destination. It looks a little like a table or a bed, and the

14

stone is worn smooth from years, perhaps centuries of use. There is a tree-trunk-sized post at the head and foot of the table.

The villagers lay me down on the stone and attach my bound wrists and ankles to the posts, then withdraw, all but one. I'm a little surprised when I recognise in the moonlight the face of the kind elderly man whose home I was sleeping in. He bends over me with a sharp knife in his hand, and I can see the old puckered tiger claw scars on his face that clearly identify him.

As he brings the blade toward my face, I have a moment of returning panic, but he only uses the knife to cut the rope that holds the gag in my mouth.

When I can speak again, I ask him, 'Why are you doing this to me?'

'You came here following the legend of the tiger goddess. Tonight, you will see her. It is a great honour, son. If you are alive in the morning, we will release you.'

I can't think of anything to say to that. It's just too far outside of the realm of any kind of reality I know.

'Listen,' the dark-skinned wizened man says.

And I do. In the distance, a tiger's roar echoes, and the other night creatures go silent out of respect.

'She comes.' The old man disappears back up the trail.

'Wait! Come back!' I shout, but he is gone in a moment. My own shout echoes in the silence of the jungle.

The tiger's roar is my only answer.

'Don't leave me out here!' I shout in futile rage as loud as I can at the old man who is long gone.

And the tiger shouts back, closer now.

I struggle against the ropes, working my wrists, trying desperately to get free. One wrist is a little looser than the other. I fight with it, wriggling and pulling. The rough ropes scrape my skin, but I am far from free.

A low throaty rumble sounds from the trees to my right.

I freeze, an instinct from generations past, as if stillness

15

will keep the predator from noticing me.

I can see the jungle foliage move as something large and quiet pushes through it. I catch a glimpse of ghostly white striped fur. A white tiger. The tiger goddess legend is about a white tiger. I could have gone to the zoo to see one, or watched Siegfried and Roy in Las Vegas a few years back. I didn't have to travel half way around the world just to end up as a white tiger's dinner.

Frustration and irritation briefly become stronger than fear. I struggle with the ropes again for a moment.

Then I look over to see where the tiger is. A great cat's eyes reflect the moonlight through the jungle greenery. I look at the tiger. And the tiger looks at me. It's nothing like the zoo. This tiger is free and in its home. I am the one who does not belong. 'Hello, tiger goddess. I'm sorry to intrude on your hunting. It was not my intention.'

The tigress blinks, and the reflective eyes disappear. The big cat moves into the shadow of a tree. No plants between me and her now, but there is only enough light for me to see the shadowy silhouette of the magnificent animal, darker blackness in the deep shadow.

And then something happens that must be a trick of the darkness and moonlight. The silhouette changes. One moment I'm looking at the dark outline of a big jungle cat, and the next the outline is smaller, more curvaceous. It becomes the outline of a woman, crouching in the leaf floor of the jungle.

I blink, thinking the light must be playing tricks on me.

A nude woman walks out of the shadow and into the light of the full moon in the clearing.

She is tall and lean, magnificently muscled like an athlete in top condition, but with breasts and hips that are beautifully full and round. Her skin is paler white than mine, and her mane of shoulder length wavy hair is a strange silvery white blonde. Her eyes lock with mine in the same steady stare that the tiger's eyes had.

16

Her eyes are no more readable than the cat's. Cold, distant, hungry. The eyes are human now, but the look on her face is not.

Doubt fills my mind, just for a moment. It's a trick the villagers are playing. It's a stage illusion. There is no way I just saw a tiger turn into a woman.

Then the woman's head tilts slightly to the side, studying me as felines are wont to do, and the moonlight reflects in her eyes like a cat's, and a trickle of rumbling growl comes from her throat.

I swallow hard. It's real. This is the legend I travelled halfway round the world to see, in the flesh. A sense of awe fills me. I am in the presence of a living myth.

She approaches slowly, teeth bared in a snarl nothing like a human smile, hands up in a defensive position as if she fears I will attack her. She growls again and circles the stone table, so that I must strain my neck to keep watching her. She moves with an almost boneless grace, as if flowing barefoot across the uneven jungle ground were the most normal natural thing for anyone to do.

She snarls and growls and makes aggressive swipes in the general direction of my bound body.

I can do nothing either to defend myself or reassure her that I am not a threat.

She leaps up onto the base of the stone table, near my feet. Crouched over me, she snarls and slaps my leg hard, making me jump and flinch.

At my movement, that inhuman tiger growl rumbles impossibly from her chest.

I freeze as still as possible.

On hands and toes she crouches down and puts her face next to my leg, eyes watching warily. She sniffs my skin, barely touching my inner thigh with her nose.

While I struggle to remain completely still, so as not to startle her, my body has a completely natural male reaction to a beautiful naked woman touching my thigh with her

17

face.

It catches her attention. She looks at my erection for a moment, looks back at my face and growls warningly, then sticks her face right in my crotch. It's definitely not a human sort of thing to do, but I can't help but have a very human reaction. I get harder, and feel chills of excitement up my spine.

She inhales my scent deeply, and nuzzles her cheek against my balls a little.

'Um, ma'am, I usually prefer to take a lady to dinner first,' I comment, intensely embarrassed as well as excited.

I should learn when to keep my mouth shut.

She growls deep and loud, a tiger's roar from a woman's mouth, and pounces on top of me, attacking my chest and face with hard open handed slaps.

I try to protect my face by raising my elbows on either side. My wrists bound to the post do not allow me to pull my arms down to protect anything else. I struggle frantically with the bonds, and am able to partially slip one hand down lower in the loop that holds it.

The more I struggle to get free, and to protect myself, the angrier she gets. Her slaps become hard enough to bruise, and I hide my face behind my upper arms as best I can.

She grabs my elbows and slams them down wide against the stone. My head and throat are unprotected. I fight against her, but she is too strong.

My struggling excites her, making her growls louder, more intense.

I stop for a moment when I realise that, and she stops, too, still holding my arms flat against the stone where I can barely move.

Her face is above me, her silvery hair backlit by the moonlight. The curve of her cheek and full lips and nose are plain for me to see. They look like Indian features, but in shades of pale white and silver. I don't think it's a trick of the moonlight. Her skin really is nearly as pure white as the bleached linen sheets I slept on at the hotel in New Delhi. One eye is lit by the moon and looks normal and human, a light color, probably gray or blue. The other is in shadow, and reflects red, which is definitely not normal or human.

The whole of her face is beautiful beyond anything as mundane as simple humanity. She is a goddess. I understand why the village elder said it was a great honour to be given to her. Even if I die tonight, to have been touched by this beauty out of legend is an experience worth all.

As I study her, she studies me with the same curiosity and even a hint of the same desire.

'Who are you?' I whisper, as softly as I can, hoping not to frighten her into another attack.

She blinks, and growls again. But her face comes closer to mine, close enough to touch my cheek with hers, very lightly. She inhales the scent of my skin, and I can feel her breath caressing me.

Perhaps she cannot speak. Perhaps the mind behind the woman's bright eyes is the mind of an animal. For some reason that thought disappoints me.

'Nayana,' she says, in a voice deep and breathy, like a whisky and cigarette singer.

I blink in surprise.

'I am Nayana,' she says again, in accented English. Not only can she speak, but she speaks my language.

'I'm David,' I say.

She growls again, that rumbling deep tiger growl that could not possibly come from a human throat. 'I did not ask,' she says.

She releases one of my arms and uses that hand to pull my face to one side, baring my throat. I can no more fight her strength than I could the strength of the tigress she was a few moments ago.

Her breath caresses along the sensitive skin of my bare neck and shoulder. She inhales deeply the scent of my skin.

19

'You smell good,' she comments.

Her tongue darts out and licks lightly on my throat. 'You taste good,' she says. Her mouth closes on my flesh, not gently. I can feel her teeth hard on my skin and her mouth sucking as if she would taste my blood, but her teeth do not pierce.

The feeling is intensely exciting, and considering the woman's dual nature, also terrifying. I have no doubt judging by the strength of her hands that her teeth could easily close through my flesh and tear my throat out like her tigress counterpart. But I can do nothing about it. If she is going to kill me, then I will die. I am helpless against her.

I lie very still in her arms, as a shiver of intense fear and excitement raises goose bumps over my entire body. My breath comes fast, and a small sound I do not recognise escapes my mouth. Fear or passion. I'm not sure which. Both, probably.

She growls again through her teeth that still touch my flesh. Her body shifts, no longer on hands and knees over me, she brings her body down on top of me. I can feel her curves and firm body and silken skin over my chest and belly. Her sex is on top of my erection, crushing it between us painfully.

I make a small movement, trying to adjust to a less painful position, and her hands tighten hard on my arm and head.

She growls right next to my ear. She takes a handful grip of my hair and yanks my head back further into a painful arch that completely exposes my throat.

Her teeth fasten on the exposed flesh hard enough to leave marks. Her hips rock above mine, rubbing her very wet sex against mine.

My breath comes fast and hard in panting gulps. I've never been so terrified or so excited in my life.

'Oh, God,' I mutter, eyes closed, as she releases my other arm and rakes her fingernails gently down my side, making me shiver. My whole body is trembling beneath her.

She licks across the skin of my throat, tasting the salt of my fear's sweat, and the hand that is not holding my head arched, with my neck exposed, wanders over my body.

She shifts a little, so that she can reach my erection with her hand. She feels it, exploring its shape, strokes it, squeezes it hard. And another small whimpering sound escapes me.

She growls and bites my throat again.

'Please,' I say softly.

'Please, what?' she asks, curiously.

'I don't know,' I say.

She chuckles softly, and it is a dark sound. Nothing of cheer. Everything of hunger.

'Are you going to kill me?' I ask and open my eyes to look at her.

She tilts her head to one side, considering. 'I have not decided,' she says. 'I am hungry and your fear smells like food.'

I close my eyes again as her tongue traces lines across my chest. She licks across a nipple and then sucks on it as it tightens, then bites on it lightly.

I arch my back and whimper again. I don't want to die, but I want her to keep touching me, so badly.

Her teeth scrape my skin, here and there. She releases my head so she can use both hands to touch me. Her fingernails dig into the skin as she grabs the muscles of my chest. She growls again, and rubs herself against my leg.

She has not killed me because she wants something else from me.

I am more than willing to give it to her. My body aches to touch her, but I am still bound and helpless.

'Let me touch you,' I say softly as I tug uselessly at the ropes.

She growls deep and angry, and I feel her teeth in my

21

belly.

'Unh,' I try to curl up to protect myself, but the ropes keep me stretched out so she can do what she pleases.

My protective reflex sets her off again. She slaps my face hard, and then yanks my head back by my hair.

'I am Nayana,' she says, eyes blazing with anger at my audacity. 'And you are food.' Her teeth bare in a snarl, and she goes for my throat, and I know, this time, I will not survive.

'Please,' I say. 'I'm sorry. Please!'

She growls low and angry, but her teeth only hold my throat, not tearing. She releases my throat for a moment. 'Please, what? What is it you beg for, human?'

'Please, don't eat me,' I say softly.

'Why?' she asks, looking at me, and there is little in her face that is human. 'You taste good.'

'Please, don't eat me, and I will serve you.'

'Serve me. How?'

'Anything. I will kiss your feet. I will please you. I will do anything you wish.'

She puts her face down close to mine again, and licks my cheek lightly. 'You taste very good.' One of her hands continues to hold my head immobile. The fingers of her other hand trace across my lips. Then she moves the hand down and squeezes hard at the joint of my jaw, forcing my mouth open.

She covers my mouth with hers, and I feel her tongue filling my mouth as her lips mash against mine. It is more like rape than a kiss, but I cannot help but moan into her mouth. How can I be so frightened and so intensely excited by the same woman? Because she is not a woman. She is a goddess, the tiger goddess, the goddess I searched the world to find. And her lips sear mine and her tongue fills me, and I moan into her mouth with need and desire.

She comes up for air in a moment. Her eyes are half closed with pleasure. She rubs her face along my throat, and

22

inhales deeply. 'Now you smell like a mate.' She growls with frustration. 'I want to eat you, and I want to fuck you.'

'Please,' I say.

And she smiles slightly, an amused expression that seems more human than any other I've seen. 'Please, eat you, or please fuck you?'

'Please, fuck me,' I say, and desire vastly overwhelms fear just at the thought that she might say yes.

She snuggles her body on top of mine again and her hips rock, rubbing her wetness along the length of me.

I shudder under her and my own hips rock in answer.

'I could always fuck you and then eat you,' she says, entirely too matter-of-factly.

I shudder again, a return of fear.

And she laughs, dark and deep. She's enjoying scaring me silly.

My face must show my realisation.

She smiles down on me, a dark wicked smile, and nods. 'I like the scent of fear. It adds spice.' Then she yanks hard on my head arching my neck back, and licks my throat. 'But don't fool yourself. I like the taste of men, and sex with a tigress is never gentle. If I choose you for a mate, you will probably die.'

I look at her eyes, and see truth in them. If she gives me what I want, it will kill me. 'What choice do I have?' I ask. I am still bound and helpless, and even if I were not, she is stronger than me. If she wants to kill me, eat me, fuck me, or kill me by fucking me, I have no say in it.

Her eyes soften for a moment. Truly human. There is a woman there, not just a tiger in a human body. 'There are few that I would choose for mate, but you are beautiful and brave.' She reaches up to the ropes holding my hands and for a moment her hands grow shorter broader and furrier. She slashes through the ropes easily with a tiger's claws. The ropes around my ankles are taken care of just as quickly.

'You have a choice,' she says, still crouched over me, as the fur disappears from her hands and arms as rapidly as it appeared, and a slim woman's hands are once again on my chest in place of a tiger's paws. 'Stay and mate with me, and know that it means death. Or go, and follow the trail back to the village.'

She withdraws until she is crouched at my feet, watching me. Her face is cold and detached, once more the impersonal gaze of the tiger.

I sit up and rub my sore wrists and watch her as she watches me. The hemp ropes rubbed me raw in places where I fought them, especially on the hand that I nearly managed to free.

A legend is crouched in front of me, a ghostly white goddess of jungle and moonlight.

I have seen tigers in zoos. So beautiful. The desire to reach out and touch them is almost overwhelming. But then they look at you with those cold eyes, and you know that if you put your arm out to touch, it will be slashed to bloody ribbons.

She is the tigress. And I want her. I want to touch her so badly, my body trembles with the desire. But her embrace is death. There is a price for touching a legend.

I came so far, drawn just by the rumours of her existence. I cannot walk away now. I will die before dawn, but in the moonlight, I will know the touch of her sweet curves, know the power of her body's strength swallowing mine.

I shift until I am kneeling in front of her.

She growls a warning.

I put my hands behind my back, vulnerable, no threat to her. And I bend, carefully down. The balance is difficult, but I dare not show her any sign of threat by moving my hands.

My lips touch her toes, and I kiss them reverently. 'Please,' I say softly, and nuzzle and lick the inner surface

24

of the arch of her foot. 'Please, do whatever you wish with me.'

She makes a soft sound, not anything like a sound a tiger would make. Very human.

I look up and see the sparkle of tears in her light eyes.

Her hands cradle my face gently, with human tenderness, and she kisses me, tender and soft, and then with increasing heat until she is all but swallowing me whole. I can barely breathe for the intensity of it.

She rubs her cheek against mine and pushes me back onto the table.

I lie under her and know that I made the right decision. This one night will be worth all my life.

She buries her face in my crotch again, and licks me and takes me into her mouth, savoring the taste and scent and texture.

The warm heat engulfs me and I feel like I'm on fire.

She moves up, her mouth, licking and nibbling across my belly and up my chest until she straddles me.

My hands lie above my head as if they were still tied. I am afraid to touch her without permission.

She grabs my wrists and pulls my hands to her breasts.

They are perfect. The firm round shapes fit my hands as if they were made for each other. I stroke and knead gently, glorying in the sweet soft skin.

She is kneeling above me, poised to impale herself on my erection.

She pulls me up into a half sitting position so that my mouth can reach her breasts.

I worship the beauty of the jungle goddess with soft kisses and the gentlest of licks and strokes and nibbles, that make her shudder in my arms.

She chooses that moment to take me into herself, and I am startled into a harder bite on her nipple than I intended.

She growls in rage and shoves me hard back onto the stone.

My head rings a little from the impact, but it doesn't distract me from the fiery heat engulfing my erection.

She leans over me and growls in my face, her hands holding my arms helpless again, as she drives her body down, forcing me to pierce her deep and hard.

I cry out from the pleasure of it, as does she, in a voice part human and part jungle cat. The villagers no doubt are awakened from their beds by the violent echoing sounds of a tigress mating.

I force my body into her deeper, rocking my hips and twisting my body, fighting her, fighting to get closer, to go faster.

She screams a big cat's ecstasy, and her body shudders and clenches on mine, and I explode inside her.

As her body bucks and shudders, it also shifts. Tiger fangs grow from her human mouth in a second, and her hands once more become paws on my arms.

I can feel the spasms of my own ecstasy as I watch her change, and I know I am a dead man. I have only seconds to live.

But the look on her human face just before it is swallowed by white striped fur is pure fiery pleasure.

I did that. I made the goddess scream with pleasure. I gave her my seed and my body and my life, and she was pleased.

And when I am dead, she will consume me, and I will be a part of her forever.

I smile into the tigress's cold blue cat eyes, as her paw comes down hard and fast on my face and throat, and her claws shred my flesh as easily as they did the ropes.

I awaken some time later. The stars are fading, so it must be near dawn. I am still lying on the stone table.

A giant cat's rough tongue strokes my face, and it hurts bad. That's what woke me.

I reach up and push the tiger's face away.

She allows it, and withdraws back to the foot of the stone bed.

I sit up, slowly, head reeling from the blow I took.

She shifts back to human form and watches me.

I reach up to my face and can feel bloody gashes along my cheek and jaw. The tiger's tongue has cleaned most of the blood, but the open wounds burn like fire.

I look at the tiger goddess, still crouching there, naked and beautiful and pure in the pre-dawn light.

'Again?' she asks with obvious eagerness.

I blink at her in surprise. I feel like I've been run over by a truck.

'Nayana,' I say, savouring the sound of her name. 'I can't.'

She digests that for a moment, blinks once and tilts her head. 'Why not?'

I laugh a little at the absurdity. 'I'm only human.'

She nods as if that is a perfectly satisfactory explanation. 'When will you be able to again?'

I start to laugh, but she's dead serious. And the goddess of the jungle may not take kindly to being laughed at, and may decide to rip my head off.

'I am not sure. A few hours? I need some rest, and food.'

She nods. 'Eat, then, and rest.' She jumps off the stone table. 'And return again tonight.'

The white tigress slips away back into the jungle night, as if she were never there.

The next week is a dream and a nightmare. Every night, Nayana demands that I return. We make love every way it is possible to make love, as many times as my body can handle. Each time, she hits me hard at the end, although after the first night, she pulls her claws, and tries to pull the strikes so they will not knock me unconscious.

It makes her impatient, waiting for me to recover.

At the end of the week, I go to the stone table, and she tells me to leave.

27

She is done with me.

A part of me is relieved. I survived the first night largely by luck, and every night since, largely by her being more careful with my fragile human self. But even so, my body is covered with bruises and scratches, and the slashes on my face will leave scars for life.

Another part of me is horrified, rejected, devastated. She is my goddess, my love. I swore to her I would serve her, even if it meant my death.

She looks at my face, and reads all that I am thinking, and feeling.

'Come back in two years,' she says softly, 'David.' It is the only time she has spoken my name. Then she is gone. The forest swallows her again.

In two years.

In two years to the day, I return to the remote village, but the goddess Nayana is dead. Poachers shot her down for her skin a week before I arrived. The villagers skinned the poachers and left their skins on the stone table. But it did not bring her back.

I go to the stone table in the jungle, and I fall to my knees and weep beside it. My life has been little more than empty waiting for two years. I was touched by a goddess, and I wear her mark. I had thought to serve her until I died. Instead, I find that she is dead. If I had been here… If I had come back sooner…

I hear a soft low rumble from the jungle. I look up into a white tiger's blue eyes. But they are not the eyes of a full grown tigress. They are the eyes of a less than half grown cub.

The cub is more than a hundred pounds, plenty big enough to make a meal of a mere human, and looks hungry, ribs showing from lack of proper nutrition, but I have no fear.

The cub changes shape as I half expected, and a small

28

skinny child stands in her place. She looks like a child of four or five, but I know she cannot yet be even two.

'Why are you crying?' the naked little girl asks curiously.

'Because Nayana is dead, and I loved her.'

'I cried, too.' The child walks up to me warily and slowly, like the wild thing that she is.

I hold very still, not wanting to startle her.

Her little hand traces the scars of a tiger's claws on my cheek. 'You are David,' she says with certainty.

'Yes, I am.'

'My mother said you would come if I waited here. I am hungry. Find me food,' she commands imperiously.

She shifts back to tiger form and rubs the side of her face against mine to mark me with her scent. Then my daughter, the little tiger goddess, curls up, purring, and places her head in my lap.

Black And White Photos
by Sommer Marsden

'What the hell is that,' I giggled into Charles's shoulder.

We stood together, arms linked, staring at the monstrosity in charcoal. Maybe that was the title, 'Monstrosity in Charcoal'.

'It's clearly... um. It most definitely is a,' he paused, stroked his chin and set his face in a scholarly mask. 'A flaming baby with three heads and a tail.'

I hid my face against his shoulder and gave into the laughter for real until he nudged me. Someone was coming. I could only guess it was someone who shouldn't see me laughing my ass off at the art.

'Ah, I see you found Caroline's charcoal of her father.' Hank slapped Charles on the shoulder and guffawed. 'Isn't it wonderful? So stark and yet inspiring such hope.'

I glanced back at the flaming, three-headed baby and smiled politely. 'Absolutely. Is Caroline here tonight?' I asked, praying the answer would be no. I most certainly hoped she hadn't witnessed our juvenile display of humour over her work.

'Sadly, no. She had to work. Even us artists have to eat. God knows, being an artist rarely pays off,' Hank said and took a healthy swig of his martini. Already his face was florid and he had that dazed, fish-eyed stare of someone well on their way to be full-on shit-faced.

30

'A shame,' I said and took Charles's arm. Hank was his friend and I had never kept my distaste for the man a secret. He had promised me the moon just to come tonight. 'We don't want to dominate your time. I know how much these art evenings mean to you. Not to mention, I saw some beautiful black and white photos over there I want to get a better look at.'

He nodded and smiled his big I-am-the-host smile. 'Ah, those were done by a new fellow. I've never invited him to art night before. Met him at a gallery opening down town. Jude Belmont. Nice boy. He's over by the shrimp puffs.' With that Hank disappeared back into crowd.

'I love how he slid in his 'art night' plug right along with calling attention to the fact that there are shrimp puffs,' I snorted as we wandered over toward the wall that displayed the black and whites.

'Be nice. He thinks he's helping his fellow artists by hosting these evenings. Who knows, he might be.' Charles patted my lower back and then surreptitiously slid his hand down for just a moment and gave my ass a squeeze. 'If you behave, I'll do something nice for you later.'

I caught his wink and grinned. It wasn't as if I had to convince my husband to have sex with me. I didn't even have to remind him to give me my due pleasure. It was him plying me with promises of sex that got me worked up.

'Well, I don't see how showing artists the work of other artists furthers anyone's career, but I will behave. Plus, I really do want to see these. I only got a quick glimpse on the way to the flaming baby, but they look like they might be rather good. Worth standing and staring at,' I said.

'Worth stroking our chins knowingly and tilting our heads?' he teased.

'Maybe so, my dear. Let's go see.'

There must have been a mad rush for the shrimp puffs then, because a wide space cleared in front of the three framed black and whites.

31

'I don't know,' Charles whispered close to my ear, 'if they're all dispersing that quickly, maybe it's black and whites of road kill.'

I started to laugh but then we were standing right in front of them and my breath caught in my throat. My pulse felt like a living thing trying to break free of my skin.

'I don't think so,' I heard myself almost sigh. 'They are gorgeous. My God, Charles, he has real talent on this wall.'

And they were gorgeous. Most certainly unexpected. In a room full of flaming babies, and still lifes of oddly shaped fruit and a few Dali-inspired melting objects, they were bright like a flame. Simple, stark, beautiful. Each was an eight-by-ten print set with a plain white mat and then framed in a brushed black frame.

The first was titled, 'Elle'. In it a tall blonde woman straddled a plain ladder-back chair. Her legs from the knees down were encased in patent leather boots. Kick-ass boots. Her wrists were encompassed in handcuffs but the chain had been broken. Her thin hands gripped the back of the chair. Her head was down, blonde hair hiding her face. With all the hair, the viewer could barely make out the studded dog collar around her neck. She looked both broken and free. I heard myself sigh again.

I moved to the second, nearly oblivious of anything but the photos. I heard Charles moving with me but even he seemed distant to me now. The middle photo was titled 'Jane'. In this one the only thing visible was the woman's face. Clearly in mid orgasm she was ugly and sensual and radiant all at once. From one angle she looked angelic, from another demonic. The distortion of her features was art in itself. Her hair was neither blonde nor overly dark. My guess was red hair. The only thing visible besides her and a swatch of nondescript bed linens was the edge of one wrist. It looked to be wrapped in fabric. Most likely a scarf. This time the sound that came out of me was not a sigh. It was more like a whisper.

As I moved on to the final frame, I noticed how damp I had grown and when Charles touched my bare wrist it was like having a match held to my skin. Every nerve was awake and alive and singing. I hissed.

'Did I hurt you?'

I shook my head, didn't look at him, and moved to stand directly in front of the final photo. 'Anna'. She was my favourite. I might have said it out loud. I don't know.

Anna had chin-length hair like me. Teacup sized breasts overrode the black lace half-cup bra she wore. Her nipples, so light in the shades of black, white, and grey, that they could only be petal pink in real life. Her hair fell around her face, hitting her jaw in a way that reminded me of a flapper. The majority of her face was swallowed by the blindfold she wore. The tip of her thin regal nose was tilted up, her lips parted in what wasn't a smile but was well on its way. She looked serene and satisfied. Behind her hair was a white pillowcase. Nothing more. Her face. The mask. The nondescript white pillow. Anna.

Charles squeezed my shoulders in his big hands and the moisture between my legs gave way to a pulsing that demanded one thing. 'I wonder what was happening to her when he took this,' I said softly so only he could hear. 'What he had done to her or was...' I let my heart still a little before I finished, 'about to do.'

'You've never been into this sort of thing,' he laughed softly in my ear. 'I think you've even used the word 'perverse'.'

'That was before I realised it was beautiful,' I said more to myself than my husband. 'Look at them. It is beautiful.' I stared at Anna again and went so far as to reach out and brush my fingers over the black frame. Could I touch what she was feeling if I touched the art? 'I wonder what was happening?' I said again and even I could hear the want in my voice.

'What do you think?' Charles asked and then his hands

were around my waist. His fingers played low over my belly. A very appropriate and marital public display of affection for anyone paying attention. Only I could feel his hard cock pressed against the seam of my ass. Only I could tell that the very tips of his long fingers brushed the very top of my pubic hair, sending tingles and frissons of energy shooting from where his fingers touched me to the tips of my toes.

'I have no idea,' I said, my voice a little harsh from the sudden overwhelming urge to fuck that had been set off in me. I loved sex, don't get me wrong, but what I was experiencing right then was the urge to rut like an animal. Irrational. Consuming. Insane. 'I wish I knew.'

'I think I know.' Charles words sent a shiver through me. Not just up my spine but through my entire being.

'Do you?' I pressed back against him. I was subtle but I did it. The feel of his cock made me close my eyes for a moment, even if it meant losing sight of the photos for an instant.

'I do. Let me take you home and I'll show you what I think.'

I nodded because I thought if I opened my mouth I might start laughing. Joy and desire and peace. That was what I saw in these photos. I didn't want to look away but I wanted to know what Anna was feeling. I knew Charles would do his best to take me there.

He broke our contact and walked away. I would simply look at them until he returned with our coats. I saw him talking to Hank. Hank pointed, chucked my husband on the shoulder and then turned to wave at me. I waved back. Then Charles was talking to another man. A younger man. Tall and thin with nearly black hair and nearly black eyes from what I could see. The man handed him a card as Charles pulled out his wallet. I saw a bill pass hands and then my husband was heading my way holding my coat and smiling.

'Who was that?' I asked as he helped me into my coat.

34

'That was the artist. I gave him a hundred dollar bill and told him to hold the photos until tomorrow. I'll go pick them up and pay him the balance.'

'How much did you pay?' I asked as he turned to me and kissed me quickly.

'Not nearly enough, I suspect,' he said and led me out.

The moment we arrived home, Charles put the blindfold on me. Technically, it was a sleep mask but it was black and it accomplished the same task. I was left on the bed, naked and in the dark. With each passing moment, my body tightened. Not with fear but with excitement and desire and the delicious feeling of being at someone's mercy. Blind to the world, my other senses were heightened. I could hear Charles's big feet padding across the hall carpet. I heard the distinctive creak of the closet in the guest room. I heard the ticking of the grandfather clock in the living room. When the chimes announced ten o'clock, it was deafening in my personal darkness.

Charles entered the room but didn't speak. That alone made my nipples rigid and the sudden harsh hardening spurred a shower of warmth through my body. I was having trouble breathing, the air seemed to have solidified. What would he do? What did he have? Would he fuck me? Eat me? Spank me? The more I thought of what he might do, the more my body responded. Becoming one hot liquid nerve.

He was at the side of the bed. Right there. I could feel him. The energy of him, and yet he didn't speak. That alone was unusual for us. Our sex was full of words and laughter and noise. His silence broke me out in goose bumps. I swore I could feel his gaze on me. Feel it like the strong stroke of hand on flesh.

My husband touched my wrist and I sucked in a breath that left me heady. My arm was raised above my head and I heard the swish of fabric before I felt the cool silk touch my skin. My wrist was bound to the maple headboard tightly but not tight enough to hurt. So, that explained the creak of the guest room closet door where I stored my rarely worn clothes and shoes. His warm hand took my other wrist and this one was also bound. Not silk this time but suede. I heard a tiny clink when he secured it. My suede belt. Thin enough to tie but the buckle gave a merry tinkle when he pulled.

'Charles.'

'Shhhh.' That was it. All he said. The muscles of my stomach tightened, fluttered, and sent a nice slow wave of warmth through my cunt. Charles never hushed me.

What had I been about to say, I wondered? Nothing. I had said his name and that was it. For reassurance? I had no idea.

His fingers started at my lips. Tracing them, pushing past gently, then forcing into my mouth and I responded. In my darkness, I responded without thinking. I took them into my mouth and sucked. I licked and nibbled and did all the things to his broad digits I might normally do to his stiff cock. He moved and when he did his erection brushed my thigh leaving a small trail of pre-come on my hot skin. The moment he moved again, I felt it start to dry.

His now wet fingers trailed down my throat. He explored the hollow of my collar bone and the sensation was overwhelming. Cut off from vision, each touch was distorted. His fingers dipped back in my mouth but only for a moment and then his wet fingertips pinched my nipples. Already erect, the sudden assault was enough to make me yelp and squirm but the dampness between my legs grew in proportion. My clitoris danced, my inner thighs grew slick.

I wanted to beg right then and there. I wanted to beg him to fuck me and fuck me hard. I knew he would. My husband would do anything and everything I asked. In my newfound darkness, Anna's ecstatic visage flashed before me. I wanted that. To feel what she felt. To see what she saw in her darkness.

36

I did not beg.

Then he was pushing his big hard cock between my lips. I gulped at it. I chased it as it bobbed before me, unable to use my hands. My mouth never stopped. Lips, tongue, teeth. I felt like I was starving and he was the only sustenance in the world. I had never wanted to have my husband in my mouth as badly as I wanted it right then. I felt greedy and ravenous and I only stopped my wet work on his cock when he pulled himself from my mouth.

The sound I made was primal. I settled only when his own wet mouth found my clit, parted my vulva, suckled and nibbled until I yanked my wrists against the gentle bonds that held me.

This is what a caged animal in heat must feel like. The thought was like an echo deep in my head that flitted out of range when his rigid tongue shoved deep into my pussy, his hard white teeth grazing my engorged clit and I bellowed as the orgasm claimed me. Behind the blindfold a kaleidoscope of colours bloomed. I yanked against my binds without thinking and the thin flesh of my inner wrists screamed with agony.

I didn't care.

And then he was in me. He had probably planned more torture but that sight, that sound. I knew my husband well enough to know that he had been pushed too far. Now he pushed into me, roughly. Stretching me, filling me and behind the mask he was all that existed. His body in my body. His cock in my cunt. His breath on my face. His hands clutching my hips and yanking me up even as he plunged into me.

I couldn't hold him, couldn't pull him closer or deeper. I was at his mercy for my pleasure and that thought started me off again. A building heat. A tightening deep inside that made me want to squirm and pant and yell. I didn't, I received. I took each harsh thrust. I absorbed the feel of his eager fingers digging into the soft flesh of my hips.

Breathed and cooed and grunted as his hairy chest slammed against my breasts and tickled my over-sensitised nipples.

'More beautiful,' he grunted and I didn't question him. My body was lighting up, flickering and moving around his. Each thrust drew me closer, each sound and grunt lifted me up and I felt it coming like a storm. I was going to come. Again. With him.

'More beautiful than Anna,' he almost yelled. His urgency was like the feel of the air after a lightning strike. So intense, so charged with energy I felt the hair on the back of my neck rise up. 'You should see yourself like this,' he growled and went rigid against me.

I came. Sobbing, babbling, pulling against my bonds to try to reach him. When he emptied into me, jittering against my body, he sounded like a stranger. Like a beast. Insane.

I shivered under him as he settled on me. Warming me.

Colours danced in my darkness. After kissing my face from forehead to chin, Charles took off the mask. I blinked feeling disoriented. He untied first the scarf and then the belt. I watched. Not speaking. Focusing on breathing.

When he turned back to me he looked worried. When I started to cry, he looked terrified.

'Did I hurt you?'

I shook my head and wiped my eyes. I felt thoroughly used and exhausted and... sacred?

He wasn't buying it and he gathered me into his arms. He smoothed and rubbed and shushed in my ear as I sniffled. 'I must have hurt you. You're crying.'

'True, but not because you hurt me.' I curled around him, feeling the pull of sleep.

'Then why.'

'It was beautiful. I can't explain.'

I felt him exhale with relief. 'It was. It really was. If you could have... you were...'

'The pictures,' I mumbled, already feeling myself drift off, 'the black and whites.'

'What about them, baby,' he whispered.
'I want to hang them in here.' My eyelids descended.
'Of course.'
'And I want to…'
'What?'
'I want to try them all,' I said, struggling.
'OK.'
'And then, I want to take our own,' I yawned. I slept.

My First Time
by Eva Hore

'Come on Doris, let's just call in and see if he's home. I'm dying for you to meet him,' Rita, my girlfriend said.

'OK. What's so special about this one? Marcus isn't it?'

'Everything. Wait 'til I show you his playroom.'

'His what?'

'Never mind. Just come on, will you?'

She dragged me by the arm up the stairs of an old warehouse that had been converted into apartments. His was on the top floor and by the time we reached it I was out of breath. She rang the bell. No answer. Rang it again, and when it still wasn't answered she took out a key.

'Why didn't you just use the key in the first place?' I asked.

'He doesn't like me barging in whenever I feel like it. If I ring twice and there's no answer, it's OK to come in and wait.'

Strange rules I thought. Either your boyfriend wanted you there or he didn't. What difference would it make if she just walked in and he was there, unless he had something to hide? Rita always met weird guys. They were like a magnet to her. This time though she said she was in love and he was very good to her.

'What do you think?' she asked, after showing me around.

40

'Nice place. What's behind that door?' I asked.

She'd shown me through the whole apartment except for this one door, painted black with a padlock on it.

'I'm not really supposed to go in there when he's not home?'

'Why, what's in there?' I said. I was intrigued now.

'It's the playroom.'

'The what? Come on, you have to show me now.'

'OK, but you have to promise never to let him know?'

'God, the way you're carrying on you'd think he had a dead body in there. Come on, show me,' I said, as she retrieved a key and began to unlock it.

Well to say I was surprised was an understatement. This room was like a dungeon. Walled in by bricks, which were painted black, and the most grotesque equipment I've ever seen. There were racks hanging from the ceiling on what looked like blocks and tackles, you know those things mechanics use to pull out motors. Ropes from the racks were attached to the wall. There was also a cage hanging from the ceiling, an iron chair without a seat, a stainless steel table, whips of different textures, and stuff that I couldn't even explain.

'What is this place?' I asked open-mouthed.

'We call it the playroom. The things Marcus does to me are unbelievable. Every week he takes me out shopping and we buy something new. I've never been so happy.'

'This is really some weird sort of shit he's got here. What have you gotten yourself into?'

'Nothing. It's fantastic. Have you ever tried it Doris?'

'No, and I don't want to.'

'How do you know if you haven't tried?' she asked.

She was rubbing herself against a wooden rack, fingering the wood lovingly. Her hand snaked around a rope, intertwining it between her fingers. Her eyes took on a glazed look as she waited for me to answer.

'It's just not my thing. I like to be in control at all times.'

'That's what I thought too, but once you've experienced this you'll never want anything else.'

I looked at her suspiciously, wondering if she was on drugs or something. I must admit I always wondered what people got out of it, but to actually participate in it with your boyfriend, and to go shopping together to buy it, well, I...

'Why don't you try it, just for a minute?' she asked.

'No, I don't think so,' I said half-heartedly.

'Let me just tie your hands together and hoist you up a little way?'

'I don't know.'

'You remember that time we bungee-jumped together? The rush you got when you were hanging upside down, knowing your fate was in someone else's hands. It really got our adrenalin pumping. Remember? It was a real buzz. Come on. No one's here to see. It's just you and me and if you really don't like it I'll untie you.'

Her face lit up as she spoke. I've never seen her so animated. She was coming closer to me with that rope still in her hands. Why not I thought. Don't knock it till you've tried it.

'OK, but don't tell anyone, all right?'

She positioned me underneath one of the hoists. Raising my hands over my head, she took the end of the rope, wrapped it around both my wrists, tied some weird arse knot that I've never seen before, and then stood back grinning at me.

She unhooked the other end of the rope, which was tied up to a bracket on the wall, and slowly pulled me upwards. The muscles in my arms shrieked as she lifted me. I was standing on the tips of my toes. Then she retied it to the wall.

'OK, is this it? Is this all you do? Hang from the ceiling?' I asked, feeling slightly foolish.

'Actually no. This is just the beginning. Imagine, your

lover is standing in front of you. He can do whatever he wants with you and there is nothing you can do to stop him.'

'I could fight him off with my legs,' I said, feeling smug.

'For how long? Your legs would tire before he did. Anyway he could tie your ankles to those ropes over there and pull your legs apart. Then you'd be at his mercy.'

I must admit the thought of it did get my pussy throbbing.

'Do you want me to show you?'

'Sure, why not, while I'm just hanging around,' I joked.

Rita tied up each ankle and slowly stretched my legs apart. Wow, the inside of my thighs and the muscles in my arms screamed out as I lifted from the ground. Rita quickly placed a box under the insides of my feet to take some of the pressure off.

'Now, how do you feel?' she asked.

'At your mercy. Yeah, I see what you mean. It is a turn on isn't it?'

'I knew you'd like it,' she giggled.

'What else do you guys do?' I asked.

'I've told you never to come in here when I'm not home,' a voice boomed from the doorway.

'I'm sorry sweetheart,' Rita cooed, 'I was just showing Doris how much fun we have together.'

'Were you now. So this is Doris. Nice to meet you,' he said, coming close to me. Coming very close. He was standing right in front of me. My pelvis was arched out towards him as though begging to be touched. I could feel myself blushing under his scrutiny.

'Er, hi,' was all I could manage to say.

'So you like playing games, do you, Doris?' he asked.

Marcus was a very sexy looking man. No wonder Rita worshipped him. He was tall, dark and handsome. Just like all the books said. He also had a body most men would die for. He was wearing all black and with his dark hair it was an irresistible combination.

'Sometimes,' I said smugly.

'Well, maybe we should initiate you into my playroom. What do you think, Rita?'

'I think Doris will enjoy it more than she knows, my love,' Rita said as he came behind her, grabbing her breasts and giving them a squeeze.

Rita was looking at me as though I was the mouse who was going to be caught in the trap. The problem was I was already in the trap and was looking forward to what was to come.

When we were teenagers, many years ago, Rita and I had fooled around a little. There was nothing much in it, especially when I thought about it now. We just fondled each other and masturbated together. There was nothing I enjoyed more than an audience. I still found that a turn on. I wondered now what else we might participate in, and how Marcus would fit into this game. I sure wouldn't mind a piece of his arse.

Marcus came closer. He had the bluest eyes, surrounded by dark lashes. When he stared into my eyes it was as though he was boring into to my soul. His face, lowered to mine. His mouth opened and his tongue dance along my lips. I nearly swooned. I opened my mouth hoping for a kiss, to feel his tongue in my mouth, but he backed away.

He brought a stool over from the corner of the room and sat on it crossing his legs. He studied me and as he did I felt as though every layer of clothing I was wearing turned invisible.

'You know what to do, Rita. Begin!' he commanded.

I hadn't paid much attention to what Rita was doing and when I looked back to where she had been I saw she had a large knife in her hand. For a second I froze, terrified of what might happen, but when she came closer she whispered for me not to worry and I relaxed, determined to enjoy every aspect of this new experience.

44

She lifted my skirt, which had hitched itself up high on my thighs when my legs had been spread, up to my waist. My pussy throbbed as her hands ran down my hips, then stole their way along the elastic of each leg until they reached my crutch. She pulled each side down, and I felt the cold steel of the knife invade my panties. I was hoping she made sure the sharp side was facing away from me. With a quick slash, the crutch opened, exposing my hot pussy

Looking to Marcus I saw he was smiling his approval at Rita. She then ripped the buttons off my shirt causing me to gasp at the suddenness of her attack. The knife then flicked under the centre of my bra and with one movement my breasts were hanging free, my bra dangling under each armpit.

I flinched at the cold point of the knife as she gently ran it around each nipple, causing them to harden instantly. My breathing was laboured, my nostrils flaring as the heat inside me grew. Licking my dry lips I watched mesmerised as Rita's mouth replaced the knife, her tongue running around my nipples. It was orgasmic.

I couldn't believe how aroused I was. My pussy was gaping through the crutch of my slashed panties, my breasts heaving under her wonderful mouth. I glanced over to Marcus, saw the smile on his handsome face, and knew what I wanted next.

But that was not to be. Rita had still not finished with me. She took a small whip from the wall and gently lashed my breasts. The sensation was tickling but that soon changed to sharp stings as she flicked me harder. She made her way down to my pussy, trailing the handle down to prod at my opening.

She replaced this with her hot mouth. Her breath tantalised me as her tongue snaked out for a quick lick. Flicking my clit with her top teeth, I moaned as her fingers entered me. I was staked out for her to do what she wished and everything she was doing was exactly what I wanted.

She finger-fucked me while her tongue worked hard on my throbbing clit.

I hadn't even noticed that Marcus had risen from his seat. He pulled her off me by the hair and threw her to the ground. He picked up her discarded whip, whipping her with it mercilessly.

'Take off your clothes at once,' he demanded.

She quickly did as asked. Standing there nude I saw bruises and whip marks from other sessions fading on her skin. She looked exquisite. She'd always been petite but now with her mature figure she looked amazing. She was totally void of body hair. Her hairless pussy reminding me of other times.

Pulling down one of the racks, he lashed her to it, arms and legs outspread. He hoisted this up high. She must have been at least four feet from the floor.

Underneath her he positioned a contraption with a huge black dildo attached to it. He lowered her gently and when she was almost upon it he rechecked the dildo and then quickly dropped her six inches or so right onto it. She let out a gasp as it disappeared inside her. Tying the rope back onto the wall he lifted a whip which must have been at least six foot long and cracked the air with it. It sounded like a shot-gun blast in the stillness of the room. My senses were electrified. I watched mesmerised as the whip licked her skin, leaving red welts behind.

'Oh, yes,' she moaned, tears streaming down her face.

He came to her then, kissing her mouth, his tongue exploring and licking her face while his hand flicked on a switch and the black dildo started vibrating inside her. Her mouth sucked back at him, her tongue reaching out to lick him as he pulled back and stared at her.

With my pussy throbbing, I watched him move over to a desk and from inside one of the drawers he took out two breast pumps. Putting one on each breast he pumped hard, until her beautiful breasts were cruelly sucked into the glass. He then tied strong rope tightly around each breast. Tighter and tighter he pulled, then released them from the pumps. They were nearly purple, the nipples and skin around them shone as the skin stretched to its limit.

My own breasts were heaving, my nipples rigid. I longed for them to be touched, pulled, attacked. My pussy was still gaping open, the wetness running down the inside of my thighs. I couldn't drag my eyes away from her body. Oh, how I wanted that to be done to me.

Her hips were rotating over the dildo as he returned with another small container. On each nipple he clipped on a small vice, turning the handle to make it grip even tighter. He then attached long chains that swung as her hips moved. Rita was moaning, enjoying the treatment that Marcus was administering. She looked awesome.

Marcus kissed her and left the room.

'Rita, are you OK?' I whispered.

'Oh, God, yes, yes,' she said breathlessly.

I watched her moving her pelvis backwards, jutting her bum outward as much as she could so the head of the dildo rubbed against her clit. I listened and heard the unmistakable cry of a woman's orgasm. My pussy was aching to have that dildo inside me. I desperately needed to release my own emotions that had been building up.

We were alone for at least ten minutes before Marcus returned. He was dressed in leather briefs, boots, vest, and a studded collar completed his outfit. He ran his hands roughly over my body, slapping my thighs, hips and breasts.

I inhaled the mixture of after-shave, sweat and manliness. My head spun as he kissed the hollow of my throat, his tongue trailing down to my breasts. He took each breast into his mouth biting the nipples hard, causing me to whimper with pleasure.

He then fell to his knees, his mouth attacking my pussy. I thought I would die from longing as his fingers opened up

47

my folds, his tongue darting in and out.

'Please, fuck me,' I begged. 'Please.'

'So, you enjoyed your initiation, did you?' he asked rising, his breath thick with my scent.

'Yes, I did. Now get me down and fuck me,' I screamed.

He slapped me hard across the face. My ears rang, my eyes blazed and never in my life did I want to be fucked like I did right now, and he knew it.

He stood in front of me, teasing me by lowering his briefs, taking out his cock, rubbing it against my pussy and then putting it back again. Perspiration was dripping from me, my body screaming for release.

He untied my ankles. They cramped as I tried to ease them back together. I was still hanging a few inches from the floor. He took the front of my panties and ripped them from my body. My skirt he pulled down and I kicked it from my feet. The muscles in my arms were screaming for release. He brought his stool over and sat on it, the rope attached to my wrists still in his hand.

Slowly he lowered me down just a little. He reached out and dragged me over to him so I straddled his lap, my pussy just inches away from his crotch. My arms bent backwards, by breasts jutting forward, nipples hard, my body electrified.

Lowering the front of his briefs, he pulled out his massive, rock-hard cock and yanked me roughly onto it. Its width was enormous as my wet pussy ground into him, not stopping until I had the whole shaft deep inside me. I wrapped my legs around his back. He attacked my nipples while I rode his cock. It was the most fantastic sex I've ever had.

'Fuck him hard,' Rita screamed, the dildo still pumping. 'Fuck him.'

He pulled on the rope until I thought my arms would be wrenched from their sockets. I held on to him with my knees, not letting his cock slip away. The harder I gripped the more he pulled so it wasn't long before only his head was inside me. Then he controlled the movements by yanking the rope up and down. I was delirious as I came all over his cock.

He rose, letting go of the ropes, allowing me to fall heavily to the floor. I unravelled the rope from my wrists and rubbed my clit frantically. It throbbed, begging for more, my fingers slipping amongst my folds. He removed Rita's dildo, lowered and untied her from the rack, undid the ropes from her breasts and lay her on the floor.

Standing above her he removed his briefs, vest and boots. He lay beside her gently stroking her flesh, licking her breasts and then his tongue lingered lovingly on her pussy. I dragged my exhausted body over and joined him in ravishing her. Together we licked and caressed her battered body. I made my way down to her swollen pussy and gently licked between the folds before Marcus pulled me away.

He entered her slowly and I watched fascinated as his cock slipped in and out. Her pussy lips were so swollen, the blood engorging there as her passion escalated. She raked her nails down his back, the scratches leaving bloody welts, and then continued to tear into his cheeks. She bucked into him with renewed energy while I licked and sucked her nipples.

My mouth reached out to hers. I whispered how beautiful she was and she cried out in ecstasy, coming as my tongue found hers. We kissed and held each other, the three of us happy, contented and fulfilled.

I knew now that I would have to have a playroom of my own, and soon.

Party Games
by Jim Baker

'We can't have a party without some decent music!'

'Agreed. Trouble is, all you ever want to listen to is the Beatles.'

'We can't play bloody classical stuff at a party!'

'Why not? It's been said Ravel's *Bolero* is one of the greatest pieces of music to make love to.'

'Who's Ravel? And what's a bolero? I thought it was three balls on a stick the Indians use to catch ostriches or something?'

Katie's knowledge of geography is marginally worse than her knowledge of music.

'Ravel was a famous French composer, a bolero is a Spanish dance, and the other thing is a bolas, dumbo. Trust you to think of something with three balls!'

Katie giggled.

'All right, Judy, but don't call me a dumbo. I'm still thinking of a way to get back at you for Monday and you'll only make it worse for yourself.'

Katie and I work together, and we've been sharing a flat for two years. Despite our different tastes in music, we have a lot in common.

We both love sex, with each other, and with a wide variety of men. I love the feel of a hard cock inside me, but I must admit I've not yet found a man who can do to me what Katie can do with her tongue.

We also love playing practical jokes on each other, and last Monday I had conned Katie into appearing dressed in nothing but panties, in front of an audience of men at the office.

Not that she really minded, especially as we brought two of them home after work and had a fabulous romp on one of our king-size beds, but, as she said, it's the principle that counts, and now I'm waiting to see how she tries to get her revenge.

Saturday would be the second anniversary of our co-habitation, and we had decided to throw a party, hence the discussion about music.

Music has always been a big thing in my life – my taste is very wide, covering classical to country and western, whereas Katie scorns almost everything other than the Beatles and the Rolling Stones.

In the end we compromised, sort of. It was agreed that in the big lounge, where people could dance, we'd have her stuff and, in the small sitting room and bedrooms, we'd have mine.

'Unless I'm in a bedroom,' she said. 'Then it changes.'

'Unless! If you don't end up in a bedroom with a bloke I'll eat my knickers!'

'Almost worth going without to watch you do it.'

Neither of us were inviting a particular man to the party. As usual, it would be open house, and we looked forward to getting lucky.

The noisier sounds of the Stones had faded away, and the gentler tones of the Beatles' 'Strawberry Fields' floated through the air.

The party so far had been a letdown, except for two interesting-looking guys who had shown up about fifteen minutes earlier. Katie had grabbed one of them and disappeared with him, and a tarty-looking blonde had beaten me to the other one. They were now locked in a passionate embrace on the sofa, kissing deeply. She was massaging the front of his jeans while his hand explored beneath her skirt. A few couples were dancing. Others were deep in conversation in the corners of the room.

I got myself a drink, flopped down in an armchair, and let the music wash around me.

I had almost given up hope when a proverbial tall dark stranger arrived and stood inside the door, looking around him.

I was halfway out of the chair when Katie's voice whispered in my ear.

'He could put his tongue in my pussy anytime he liked.'

'What? Who?'

'That dark-haired hunk. Wouldn't you like him to take your panties off?'

She laughed and shoved me back into the chair.

'You have a nice rest. I'll check him out!'

'Hang on! Where's your other bloke?'

'I took him in the other room for a snog. God, that music you've got on in there is awful! Anyway, he was unhooking my bra and I'd just got his zip down when his girlfriend turned up. He saw her before she saw us, thank Christ!'

She grinned at me.

'I'll let you know if that one's any good!'

Before I could protest she had gone across the room and I saw her touch the dark guy's hand.

I looked gloomily across at the couple on the sofa. Their lips were still glued together, the girl's skirt was up around her waist, and the guy's hand was moving under the waistband of her panties. The silky material rippled as his fingers stroked. She had unzipped his jeans and her hand was searching inside.

Time dragged on, the Beatles droned on, and I was beginning to think of going to bed alone.

'Would you care to dance?' A large form bent over me, holding out a hand. He took my hand and pulled me up. 'I'm John,' he said. 'Why do you look so sad?'

He manoeuvred us into a dark corner, and brushed my lips with his.

I kissed him hard and whispered in his ear.

'I'm sad because I don't have a cock in my pussy.'

He recoiled slightly, and then laughed. 'Can I help?'

'Only if you're man enough.'

He laughed again, and turned us until my back was against the wall. 'Why don't you check?' He pulled me against him and kissed me, tongue probing. His legs parted slightly and I dropped both hands down to his cock. I squeezed it through his pants, and he gasped. Quickly I hauled the zipper down. A long, hard fleshy rod sprang into my hand, and I wrapped my fingers around it, and ran my thumb across the head as I gazed over his shoulder, across the room.

The music moved on to the slow beat of 'Hey Jude'.

The blonde girl's panties were round her knees, and the guy's cock was in her hand. I watched, fascinated, as she stroked his cock in perfect time to the music, slowly and deliberately. Her eyes were closed and her tongue licked back and forth across her lips as his fingers searched the dark patch between her thighs.

'*Some blonde*,' I thought hazily as John's hand fondled my breasts.

An Asian girl with long black hair was dancing alone in the centre of the room, gyrating slowly. She unbuttoned her blouse and let it fall. She wore no bra, and her firm, olive breasts gleamed in the candlelight as if they were oiled. She unzipped her skirt, dropped it, and danced on. Her hair swept from side to side as she swayed to the rhythm of the music.

I watched, entranced by the gorgeous figure, felt the heat between my legs, and the music swirling in my brain. John's hand moved under my skirt, up the inside of my thigh, and his fingers pulled my panties aside.

I remembered the cock in my hand and began to stroke it dreamily to the beat of Ringo's drums.

One finger slid inside me, then another. He ran the ball of his thumb over my clit, making me groan. He pulled me tighter against him and thrust his tongue into my mouth. Our rhythm matched the beat of the music and I felt my orgasm beginning as our hands and tongues moved together. His slick cock got hotter and thicker in my fingers until he gave a rasping groan and hot liquid spurted through my fingers. My body shook as I climaxed, and I shut my eyes tight and leaned heavily against the wall behind me.

When I opened them, I found I was staring directly into the wide-open eyes of the Asian girl, as she swayed to the closing chorus of 'Hey Jude'. She smiled, and I saw she had her fingers under the waistband of her panties, and was stroking herself slowly.

As I pushed myself upright and took a step toward her, a hand took mine.

'Dreaming about making sweet music with that little cutie, are you? She certainly got off watching your performance!'

Katie was barefoot, her eyes were gleaming, and her face was flushed. She was wearing a man's long shirt and nothing else.

'Come on, I've got something you'll like!'

She pulled me across the room to the stairs.

The couple on the sofa were screwing now. The girl's panties lay on the floor, and the guy's jeans were halfway down his buttocks. He was thrusting in and out of her with long, hard strokes.

Katie led me up the stairs and into her bedroom, where Beatles music was playing softly.

The dark-haired guy was lying naked on the king-sized bed, with his eyes closed. My eyes went straight to his cock. It was lying half-erect on his flat stomach. My gaze slid over the olive skin of his chest to his handsome face and curly black hair.

'This is Tony. Not bad, eh?' Katie chuckled. A pair of bright blue eyes opened, and he grinned up at us.

'So I guess you're Judy? Katie told me you two girls like to swing both ways.'

He looked from me to Katie and back.

'Well, I know she's a real redhead. Are you a natural blonde?'

'Well, Tony, Katie and I'll have some fun and you'll soon see. But first let's change the music. You look like an opera lover'

'Of course. I'm half Italian.'

Ignoring Katie's protests, I removed the Beatles CD from the music system and replaced it with Verdi's *Aida*.

As the music filled the room, I turned to Katie and held out my arms.

'Come here, baby.'

I looped my left arm around her neck, pulled her up against me, and kissed her hard. I tugged the shirt she was wearing over her head, and rolled her on to her back. She moaned as I pulled gently at the mass of red curls between her legs and let my fingers roam over the soft fleshy lips of her cunt.

'You're so wet, baby,' I whispered in her ear. 'What have you been up to?'

My lips wandered down to her breasts and I took a nipple between my teeth, bit it gently, and then sucked it, hard. Katie let out a little scream as I pushed two fingers into her cunt.

I looked up at Tony. He was nursing a huge erection and with my free hand I pointed at it and then at Katie's open mouth.

He grinned, slid across the bed and positioned the tip of his cock by her lips, put his hand behind her head and slid it into her mouth. Her eyes opened as she began to suck, and she took his cock further into her mouth. I moved down the bed and knelt between her thighs. I pushed her knees wide apart, and lowered my face into her soaking crotch.

I licked her clit, and then took it between my lips and sucked. I closed my eyes and let my senses slide until there was nothing in my world other than the glorious music in my ears and the bittersweet taste of Katie in my mouth. From far away I heard the sound of her voice.

'Go on, Tony, now!'

The mattress bounced, and I felt my skirt thrown up over my back. My panties were pulled aside, and the hot tip of a cock parted my pussy lips. Strong arms came around me, and I shuddered as fingers tweaked my nipples.

'Ready?' he said, and slid his cock inside me in one long thrust.

'Oh, fuck!' I'd realised he was big but I'd never been filled like this.

Tony settled his hands on my hips and began to ride me with slow strokes, then I heard him laugh as his tempo speeded up.

'I told you I liked opera,' he said, and I realised I was being expertly fucked to the rhythm of the Grand March in *Aida*.

Again and again his cock hammered into me and my body began to tingle. The muscles around my cunt tightened as the orgasm built and built. Bright lights were flashing in my head, and I was lost in the sensation of the music and the fantastic cock inside me.

My mouth was still buried in Katie's cunt; my tongue worked automatically and I felt her hand on the back of my head forcing me onto her harder until suddenly she screamed and hot liquid gushed into my mouth.

Tony thrust even harder, and as his finger touched my clitoris, an intense orgasm ripped through me. I heard him yell as more hot liquid pumped into my cunt until I collapsed forward, and lay flat on my stomach, exhausted.

After a few minutes I heard Katie's laugh.

'Some cock, yeah?'

I rolled over and looked at Tony, who was on his back, eyes shut.

'He deserves a rest.' I laughed.

Katie stroked my hair gently.

'Thank you for making me come,' she said. 'Come here.' She kissed me and I pushed my tongue, still coated with her juice, deep into her mouth.

'Dirty bitch,' she murmured, after sucking it as hard as she could. 'Do you want me to eat your pussy?'

'What do you think?'

'Lie down.'

She had me completely off my guard. As I turned on to my back, she straddled me, her knees on my biceps, and her crotch inches from my face.

'Get off!'

'Ask nicely, then.'

She wriggled herself a little further forward until her pubic hair tickled my chin.

'Say pretty please.'

'Bitch!'

I struggled but Katie is bigger and stronger than me, and she held me easily.

'Now that's naughty.'

She moved her crotch directly over my mouth.

'One more chance.'

I glowered at her then turned my head to look at Tony, who was propped up on one elbow watching the action with a broad grin on his face. I guessed Katie had set up this little scenario in advance, and I had a pretty good idea why.

'Cow!'

'Dear me, Judy, that's very naughty.'

She lowered herself on to my nose and mouth until I could barely breathe.

'You'll have to be punished for that.'

Her knees clamped against my ears and she let her whole weight down on my face, grinding down as I fought for breath, then lifted herself up leaving my mouth and nose full of the musky smell of her sodden pussy.

'Please let me go, Katie,' I whimpered.

'Not just yet. Now start licking, you know exactly how I like it.' Reluctantly I began flicking my tongue in and out of her pussy. 'Come on sweetie, you can do better than that. You're staying right where you are until you make me come, so work a bit harder. I'll teach you to play jokes on me.'

As I thought, this was her revenge. I brought the tip of my tongue on to her clit, and went to work. 'That's better.' Katie was beginning to breathe faster. 'Let's see which of us gets there first. Look.'

She unclamped her legs and I turned my head to see the tip of Tony's erect cock an inch from my face with Katie's hand pumping on the shaft

'I'd shut your eyes if I were you,' she said gleefully. 'He's pretty close.'

The last word came out as a groan as my tongue took her over the brink and the flood of her juice into my mouth coincided with a jet of hot semen across my eyes and nose as Tony climaxed.

I lay still with my eyes closed and felt Katie's weight lift off me.

'Wipe your face, darling,' she said and a piece of cloth was pushed into my hand. I wiped the sticky goo away and opened my eyes to see the cloth was a pair of men's underpants, presumably Tony's. I hurled them away, and the other two laughed.

'I think we're even, Judy,' said Katie. 'Why don't you take a shower?'

I stood up from the bed without a word and stalked into the bathroom. As I closed the door I her voice murmuring, 'Come on big fellow, let's see if we can get that cock hard again.'

I pulled off my damp, wrinkled skirt, turned the shower on full, and stepped inside. The hot water pummelled me and I rubbed shampoo vigorously through my hair. I stood under the hot water for a long time, soaping myself and watching the mixture of sweat and love-juices swill away down the drain. Then I towelled myself dry, wrapped a towel around me, and went back into the bedroom.

The Rolling Stones' 'I Can't Get No Satisfaction' had replaced Verdi, but hardly seemed to fit the antics on the bed.

Tony certainly had good powers of recovery, to my knowledge he had come twice in the last hour and, if Katie was to be believed, once just before that. Now her legs were draped over his shoulders, and she was digging her nails into his back as he pounded into her again. Both of them were wholly oblivious to my presence.

I wandered down the stairs into the lounge. Rolling Stones music was playing there as well. Half empty glasses and wine bottles were strewn around and at first I thought everyone had gone until I saw the couple on the sofa, still locked in each other's arms, sound asleep.

I changed the music to Beethoven, poured myself some wine, slurped it down and poured some more. I slumped into a chair, and drank the second glass slowly, thinking about the games upstairs, and then laughed. Katie had won this round but my time would come.

The next thing I knew a hand was shaking me gently.

'It's OK, it's Tony. Katie's asleep. I'm off, thanks for some great music, and everything else.' He grinned. 'Tell Katie I'll ring her.'

I looked at the clock and saw it was four-thirty. The couple on the settee had woken when Tony spoke, and started to make love again, so I left them to it and went back upstairs.

Katie was lying naked, sound asleep on the middle of the bed, arms and legs flung out like a starfish. It was far too good a chance to miss.

I opened her lingerie drawer and found two pairs of nylon stockings. I knotted two through the headboard and tied the other two to the base of the bed, making as little noise as possible. Then, very carefully, I tied the other ends loosely on to Katie's wrists and ankles.

Katie started to wake as I tightened the knots on her wrists, but she was still groggy, and I had enough time to fix her ankles as well. She struggled frantically, but soon gave up and lay back, glaring up at me.

'My turn, sweetie-pie,' I said, dropping the towel. 'I'll be gentle with you. But first…'

I put the CD of Ravel's *Bolero* on the music system.

'Now baby, you'll see why this is great music for sex.'

I pressed the 'start' button on the remote control and – as the first, soft strains of the music filtered into the air – I began to play with Katie's body.

I started on her breasts, licking and sucking the nipples until she was breathing hard, then I moved down to her cunt. I played with her pubic hair, tickled the swollen lips of her vagina, and slipped my fingers in and out of her until she whimpered. My finger flickered over her clit as the rhythm of the *Bolero* built up steadily and I brought her nearer and nearer… then took my hand away and at the same time I stopped the music.

'Jude, please don't stop!'

She struggled against the bonds, desperate to get her fingers on her pussy and bring herself to climax while I sat and watched.

She came down slowly. I started the music again from the beginning and just as slowly brought her back up towards the brink with my fingers, a little nearer this time. As her body began to tense I picked up the remote control again and grinned down at her.

'Guess what?'

After the fourth time she was weeping tears of frustration as she begged me to let her come.

'Not yet, darling,' I said. 'You were greedy tonight, pinching both men. Are you still ticklish?'

A look of panic crossed her face. Katie wasn't just ticklish; she was ultra-ticklish, to the point where tickling her would make her hysterical. I had watched once as two guys had held her down and tickled her at a college party. I thought she was going to die as she giggled, and wept, and screamed for mercy.

'Please no, Judy. Don't tickle me. Come on, I'll eat you. I'll make you come as many times as you want.'

'Too late.'

Once more I started the music, further into the CD this time, where the persistent beat was louder and faster.

Her body went rigid as I straddled her across her waist, and placed my fingertips on her rib cage. She screamed as I put them to work, tickling up and down her ribs. The giggling started and turned to shouts of laughter as I worked up under her armpits and down again. Her body jerked and thrashed and tears streamed down her cheeks as I wriggled my hands under her knees and up and down the insides of her thighs, then back to her ribs again.

'Please stop,' she gasped, again and again. 'I'll do anything you want.'

At last I stopped, and she lay limp, gasping for breath.

'No more, Judy, please.'

'Just one last time. Where are you really ticklish, Katie?'

I knelt at the bottom of the bed.

'Oh God, no, Judy – not my feet. Please don't tickle my feet. I'll go mad.'

I ran the fingernail of a little finger up the sole of her right foot and her body jerked as if it had received an electric shock.

'Please don't!'

The *Bolero* was moving towards its climax and the sounds of the brass shrieking and drums pounding crashed through the room

I did the same to the other foot with the same result.

'You are a sensitive little girl, aren't you? Are your feet more sensitive than your clit? Let's see.'

I knelt on her thigh, pinning the leg down, and positioned myself so I could reach her foot with one hand and her cunt with the other. I played with her clit, and her rigid body relaxed. I pushed two fingers into her cunt and thrust them in and out, rolling her clit with my thumb. Her orgasm came closer and closer, and this time I had no intention of stopping.

Her climax coincided with the last screaming chords of music, and, as I felt her going over the top, I ran all four fingertips rapidly up and down the sole of her foot. Her body bucked and reared, she babbled incoherently, and then slumped down heavily on to the sheets.

After a long time she opened her eyes.

'Christ, I've never come like that,' she whispered. 'I

blacked out. I thought I was going to die.'

'I told you the music was good!'

'Untie me, baby. I must go to sleep.'

As the sunlight trickled through the window, we dropped off to sleep in each other's arms.

I'll have to keep my eye on her though – she'll want her revenge.

Dangerous Games
by Eva Hore

My boyfriend and I have just started acting out new sexual experiences. Today he sent flowers to me at work. On the card, scribbled in bold print, was a message, *Bedroom at six o'clock sharp. No peeking before then.* Giggling I put the flowers in a vase on my desk and told my best friend, Carmen, what David was up to. She told me I had to report every detail to her the following day.

'So what is it?' I asked, when he finally picked up the phone.

'I take it you received my flowers?' he said, ignoring my question.

'Yes, and they're beautiful,' I said.

'Not as beautiful as you,' he whispered.

'Are you going to tell me what you're up to?' I asked.

'No,' he said, 'and I don't want you ringing me all afternoon. Just do what I ask and, I guarantee, this is one night you'll never forget.'

'OK,' I said, with my pussy beginning to throb. 'I'll see you at six.'

On the way home in the train, I couldn't help but smile. An old lady sitting across from me smiled back. She would have died had she known what I was thinking. David's cock and what he could do with it was consuming my thoughts.

At two minutes to six I entered the bedroom to find a

package in the centre of the bed. Excitedly ripping the paper to shreds, I found inside a sexy red teddy, suspenders, stockings, a red silk scarf and a note.

The note said that I was to change into the underwear, blindfold myself and wait patiently on the edge of the bed. I stripped my clothes off quickly, inching up the teddy which was high cut on the leg and very low in front, exposing most of my breasts. The stockings were silk, and as I hooked them into the suspenders I glimpsed myself in the mirror and knew David would like what he saw. Painting my lips with bright red lipstick, I looked like a sexy vamp, just the effect I wanted. Adjusting the teddy and posing on the bed to look as alluring as possible, I blindfolded myself and waited, anxious for him to arrive.

My body was becoming stiff and my legs were cramping before I heard the door slowly creak open. Finally! I was beginning to wonder if this was going to turn out a practical joke. Footsteps came closer. I sensed his presence near the end of the bed. Neither of us spoke. The silence only heightened my desire as I sat there waiting for him to begin.

Finally, I asked, 'David, is that you?'

He didn't answer.

'David,' I said again, giggling to overcome some nervousness. It flashed through my mind that perhaps it wasn't him at all, and I was sitting, practically naked, in front of a stranger, begging to be fucked. I realised that this was probably how David wanted me to feel. He was always saying it was healthy to fantasise, because the action was going on in your head and you weren't hurting anyone.

So I sat patiently, imagining a complete stranger, perhaps a burglar, standing before me. This man would probably wonder why I was wearing a blindfold and sexy teddy, and what I was waiting for? It would have been obvious that no one else was at home. He might contemplate stealing some sexual favours from me before helping himself to some of our other possessions.

I was smiling slightly, toying with the idea when a hand on my shoulder pushed me back on the bed. Licking my lips, I lay there excited, titillated by my own thoughts. As he shifted his weight onto the bed I rolled towards him, and I noticed he was wearing a different aftershave. The sly dog really was trying to confuse me.

My breath caught in my throat as ice cold fingers pushed me back over and then slid under my straps, lowering the top of the teddy down, exposing me. Goose bumps prickled my flesh as the fingers lightly danced over my breasts, pinching the nipples and then trailed up my neck and around my chin only to run across my lips, before entering my mouth.

I sucked on them lightly, knowing that in my fantasy I would really be afraid at this point and would fight off an unknown stranger. I moved my head sideways, not wanting to continue but the fingers came back and this time a hand held the back of my head firmly, pushing and pulling me, backwards and forwards, demanding they be sucked.

For a moment I was frightened but then I sucked them in deeply, rolling my tongue around and as the hand released my head I sucked at them as though enjoying a frozen ice-cream.

Then like a jolt of electricity I felt cold circling my nipples. Ice was being massaged over them and they stiffened instantly as trickles of water ran down my sides. A hot tongue lapped at the water and worked its way to the very edges of my breasts.

I gasped in shock when more ice, now in the palm of his hands, caressed my breasts as well. My body was hot and excited as more ice melted and trickled down. My pussy began to contract and a deep throbbing grew inside me. Then his hot mouth covered my breasts and licked me lovingly, replacing the cold with heat.

The sensation was amazing. I arched my back so he could get as much of my breast as possible into his mouth.

He nibbled my nipples that were erect from the cold, teasing and licking them and, just when they'd returned back to their normal temperature, he slipped more ice into his mouth. The heat from his mouth melted the ice quickly. It was amazingly erotic and I opened my legs letting him know I was ready for some action.

I imagined a strong young man, stealing this most private of possessions, my body, as he sucked and licked. Then his tongue travelled to my mouth to kiss me. I reached up to hold his head in my hands but he slapped them away, pinning them together above my head with one hand while the other travelled down my body.

I opened my legs wider, my pussy throbbing with desire, grinding my pelvis up as his hand ran over my mound. I wanted him now. I'd already had enough of this game and was concentrating on his cock entering my pussy when suddenly a cold piece of ice was slipped into my mouth. As our tongues entwined it melted from the heat we generated together.

His teased his tongue from my mouth and with the tip of it he touched the underside of my lip, tormenting me until ice replaced his tongue and water trickled out of my mouth and down my chin. He licked at it, lapping it up as it dribbled out of the sides of my mouth and into my ears.

He shifted his weight, releasing my hands and I was hoping he was going to finally satisfy my aching pussy. It was the most erotic experience, being blindfolded and not being able to see what was going to happen next.

For a few minutes he did nothing. I wasn't sure where he was. He could have been staring at my pussy as I lay there with my legs wide open, or he could have been surveying the room for what to steal. I gasped out loud, then giggled as more ice hit my midriff. His hand cupped it as he massaged it over my abdomen and down to my pubic hair. He slipped his hand inside the teddy and rested it over my hot pussy. The ice melted instantly and dribbled down my slit, just touching my hole.

God, I'd had enough! I wanted David now. I wanted his cock inside me so I squirmed towards him, holding his hand there, trying to force his finger inside so he could see how ready I was.

'Please,' I begged, not caring if in my fantasy I would be demanding a complete stranger to make love to me. All I knew was at that moment I needed a cock, regardless of whose it was.

I made to sit up, to remove the blindfold, but I was pushed back and my fingers slapped away. Sexually frustrated I lay back down, breathing hard. Suddenly, sharp slaps stung my thighs.

'Hey,' I complained, not used to such rough play. Instead of stopping he continued slapping and my protests quickly turned to pleasure as I began to enjoy this unusual turn of events. David was always a considerate lover and now I enjoyed the excitement of being smacked while blindfolded, allowing him to act out a fantasy of his own.

Fingers were at my pussy. Finally I was going to get what I wanted. Roughly, the crutch of the teddy was flicked open and I arched my back, pushing my pelvis upwards as I opened my legs, inviting him in, while whimpering for his cock.

Almost feather-like the tip of his tongue touched my clit. I thought I'd faint from longing. Again and again he flicked it, then his teeth nipped at it. It was exquisite. Now his tongue was roaming through my folds, on and on he licked until I closed my legs tightly around his head, holding him there.

He pulled back and I anticipated his huge cock entering me, but instead I felt the stinging pain as my teddy was ripped from my body. He tore my stockings from the suspenders and I lay there shocked and excited as his hands were roaming all over me at once.

'Oh, David, please let me take the blindfold off,' I

begged.

Again for a few minutes he said nothing as I lay there exposed, my pussy gaping, my legs quivering, my breathing erratic. He lifted both my arms above my head, his hands running down my arms, over my breasts, down my abdomen and then he was holding me by the hips, as he positioned himself between my legs.

'Fuck me, David, just hurry up and fuck me,' I begged.

My pussy was numb from the ice and my body was electrified with passion. Water had pooled on the bed, saturating the sheets. Then he was kissing me and the next thing I knew his cock was inside me. I actually didn't feel its presence until after he had entered, my lips still numb from the ice.

The sensation was amazing as he fucked me, slowly easing in and out as his cold hands massaged my breasts. Because my pussy was so numb it was easy for me to imagine this wasn't David. Dangerously, I let my mind continue on with the fantasy that this was a stranger who was fucking me. My hand stole down, wanting to grab hold of his cock but he slapped it away.

I was moaning and writhing around the bed. The sensation of extreme cold and then heat was magical. I opened my mouth to ask if I could take the blindfold off as I wanted to watch his cock going in and out, but instead his hot tongue thrust into my mouth and I bucked wildly enjoying the combination of cock and tongue.

I wrapped my legs around his back and pushed my pelvis into him, gyrating and twisting, feeling warm water ooze from my pussy while his fabulous cock picked up my tempo.

With our tongues exploring each other's mouths and my whole body electrified, I came with the most earth-shattering climax ever, one that left my body sensitive and tingling all over. I heard him gasp as my orgasm gushed around his cock to mingle with the watery ice in a pool on the bed.

Fulfilled and completely drained, I collapsed back on the bed, but he was thrusting into me harder now, lifting one leg high, fucking me like never before. I could hear him gasping as his breath expelled loudly with every thrust he made, and then he too came, moaning as his hot seed shot deep inside me.

He collapsed on top of me and we both lay there panting. I imagined the burglar was the one lying prostrate on me. I envisaged David coming through the door, tearing this man from me and beating him to a pulp, while I lay there defenceless and naked.

At some stage David got up and I must have slipped into a light sleep because the next thing I remembered was hearing a mobile phone ringing as though far away. It took me a while to realise it was mine. I was still blindfolded and naked on my bed.

Tearing the blindfold off I groped for the phone, which was in my handbag, near the bed. Finally, I answered only to hear David on the other end.

'Darling, I've been worried sick. Where have you been?'

'What?' I said.

'I've been trying our phone for over an hour. I wanted to explain why I couldn't make it. Are you OK?'

I looked over towards our phone and saw it was off the hook. What was David saying? He couldn't make it… Then who had made love to me?

'Melissa, are you alright?'

'Yes,' I mumbled, stalling for time. 'I fell asleep waiting.'

'Good, then you'll be nice and refreshed. I'll be home soon,' he said.

I hung up the phone in a daze, looking about the room. Nothing seemed to be missing. My teddy was ripped and lying discarded on the floor. The bed was a mess and as I peered down at my body I noticed some bruises where he'd been too rough.

Who had been rough?

Had it been David and now he was pretending he hadn't been here at all?

Or had it really been a stranger?

What was I to do? If I told David and it hadn't been him then he'd been furious, and if I didn't tell and it was him he'd always think I kept things from him.

I hurried about the room straightening it up. I'd already decided what I'd do. I'd quickly shower, lay on the bed, naked, and cuff my legs wide open. This was something I allowed David to do on occasions because it turned him on so much. Then I'd not only blindfold myself but I'd put a gag in my mouth before I locked my wrists into the handcuffs.

I'd dim the lights and lay there vulnerable for him and hope he'd attack me with relish and maybe, just maybe I'd never have to explain where the sexy negligee had disappeared to.

Fantasy
by DMW Carol

I was thinking about costumes… I wonder if he likes school uniforms? Maybe it should be something like that, my short black skirt, some nice black undies – panties, stockings, suspenders and a lacy bra, with a tight white shirt over the top and that school tie.

What would he do if he got home and found me dressed like that, lying across my bed reading Harry Potter with a teddy bear tucked under one arm and an enormous lollipop in the other hand? I hope he'd love it. It would be fun to pretend to be sweet and innocent for a change. Well, maybe not too innocent.

I'd make my eyes as wide as possible, then look up at him and tell him that I was really sorry for letting myself into his room, but someone had told me that he could teach me how to make love to a man and I wanted to learn. Then I'd ask him to be really gentle with me because I've never done anything like this before and I'm a bit scared, which is why I want to learn from an expert.

Then I'd just gaze adoringly at him and lick my lollipop while he decided how to respond. Maybe I'd play with my hair and try to look shy… if he didn't come over and kiss me, I'd ask him what I needed to do to be pretty enough that a man like him would want to kiss me.

I'd pretend not to know how to kiss properly and ask

him to show me, letting him teach me how to open my lips and let his tongue brush over mine. I'd have to ask if I was doing it right. Then maybe I'd let my arms slip around him so he started to stroke and caress me, running his hands over my shirt, showing me where it was going to feel nice and getting me to tell him which touches felt the nicest. Then he could tell me to do the same to him, telling me to run my hands over his shoulders and his chest, letting me feel the lovely warmth of his skin, telling me when and how it felt good, sometimes asking me to stroke harder or just use my fingertips and all the time his hands would be exploring me, stroking my back, maybe even scratching along my spine or slipping lower to brush over my thigh and trace around the tops of the stockings.

I'd wriggle in close to him so he could feel my breasts pressing against his chest and couldn't resist giving them a gentle squeeze or two, crushing me close to him and telling me that he could tell that he'd be able to teach me how to become a fantastic lover by the way I was responding to his touch and the fact that my kisses were turning him on so well. Maybe he would grab my hand and move it down so I could feel how rigid his cock was getting.

I'd pretend that made me feel really nervous, of course, that I wasn't expecting anything so big and hard, so he'd have to promise that it wouldn't hurt if I was really turned on first. Then he could explain how he needed to do things to make my pussy wet enough so it didn't hurt... he could ask if I could feel it getting wetter while he stroked me and kissed me and then maybe he'd tell me that it would work better if he undid my shirt. Mmmmmm, I think he'd have to take my shirt and bra off and then pay lots and lots of attention to kissing and licking and sucking on my nipples, telling me to feel how wet I was getting while he did it. Then he'd have to peel my panties off so he could test how wet I was, just running one finger over my pussy so I was shivering at his touch.

73

Maybe he'd tell me to feel how wet I was getting myself, he could place my hand in just the right place and tell me how to part the lips and start exploring inside. Then maybe he would slip one finger inside me and tell me that he could tell by how easily it goes in now that I'm ready to be fucked. I'd tell him that it felt really good, but I was still scared because his cock was much bigger than his finger.

Then I'd tell him I'd never seen a cock before and ask him to step out of his trousers so I could have a good look, I bet he'd be really hard too, standing to attention all long and hard and swollen… I'd ask him if all cocks were this big and hard and then carefully reach out to run a finger over it and feel the ridges and veins on the surface.

He'd have to show me how to hold it properly, maybe holding his hand over mine and stroking it along the full length of his shaft, squeezing my hand so I held him just tight enough. He'd have to tell me how good it felt, and get me to try stroking him at different speeds and holding tighter or looser so I could feel exactly what a cock was like.

One of us would point out the pre-cum leaking at the top and suggest that I should taste it. He'd have to tell me that it was safe and wouldn't hurt me, of course, and that if I really want to please a man I have to know to make his cock happy with my mouth as well as my hand. I'm sure he could talk me into trying a taste though, just flicking my tongue over the tip. He'd ask how it tasted and I'd tell him it was a funny taste, kind of salty and slightly bitter but a bit sweet too.

I'd taste a little more, this time pressing my tongue harder against him and letting it caress him while I licked. He could tell me whether I was doing it right or not, suggest I took him into my mouth or licked lower, slower, faster or whatever he fancied. He could tell me to hold him at the same time, or use my hand to stroke his balls or squeeze his bum or even have me slip a finger inside his arse while I sucked and licked to his exact instructions. He would have to tell me when I was getting it right and encourage me to keep trying harder. He could tell me to keep on sucking him until he came in my mouth, or stop and let me watch while he showed me how he stroked that wonderful cock of his so his come sprayed all over me.

Then he'd tell me that I'd already learned a lot, but there was more I needed to know. The next lesson was how to receive pleasure because it is impossible to be a good lover unless you're really really enjoying what you're doing. Then he'd tie me to the bed and blindfold me so all I was aware of was the sensations. He'd tell me to just relax and let him show me how good making love could feel.

First he'd start by stroking and kissing me all over, telling me how wonderful I felt and tasted, he'd spend ages playing with my breasts, licking and sucking and nibbling at my nipples until I was moaning with pleasure. He'd tell me that it was going to get even better and then slide one hand down my torso until his fingertip was just circling my clit. Then he'd explain to me that the clitoris is the most sensitive spot on a woman's body, maybe he'd flick it with a fingernail so I jumped at the sensation or rub it so hard I felt like I was going to explode and then go back to soft slow gentle circling so I was intensely aware of every movement. He'd move lower until I could feel his breath on my pussy, maybe letting his hand work a little lower so one finger was just inside me, just the tiniest fraction inside but enough to make me tingle all over.

He'd lick my clit as his finger slipped properly into me, telling me how much I was going to love this lesson. It would feel so wonderful that I wouldn't be able to resist moaning a little and begging him to teach me more. Maybe he'd add a second finger inside me and start curling them and letting them bounce against the top wall of my pussy, teasing my G-spot, licking me at the same time or nibbling and sucking on my clit until I was almost screaming in ecstasy. He wouldn't stop until I'd come for him, long and hard and making me shake all over at the intensity.

Then he'd move up to kiss me and tell me that he'd bet I had no idea that anything could feel that good. I'd tell him that it was wonderful, incredible, fantastic and thank him over and over again for being such a wonderful teacher. Then he'd begin slowly stroking me again and telling me that now I was ready for the next lesson... he'd tell me it was time I learned how to be fucked.

I'd pretend to be frightened by this, claim that after seeing him come and then having such an incredible orgasm myself I'd thought it was all over. I wanted it to be all over.

But he'll tell me 'no'. There was no way he was going to have a naked little slut tied to his bed and not give her a damn good fucking. When I objected more, he'd climb on top of me and rub his cock between my tits telling me that there was no point objecting because, like it or not, his cock was going to be inside me any time now. I'd watch him growing hard on top of me and beg him to stop, I'd offer to suck him, again or do anything else he wanted if only he didn't fuck me. He would laugh at me and tell me that I was going to do anything he wanted anyway. I'd be so excited that I could hardly keep still, arching against him even as I pretended to say no, encouraging him to be rougher with me now, squeezing my tits hard enough that they hurt, leaving scratch marks as he clawed at them. He'd tell me to lean up and lick his cock and when I didn't he'd slap it against my face until I could no longer resist. Maybe he'd grab a vibrator and hold it against my clit to make sure I stayed wet for him, grinding it against me so hard that I couldn't tell whether I was feeling pain or pleasure.

When he was ready he'd kneel between my legs and force his cock into me as hard as he could, pushing it so deep inside me that I felt that it would never come back out. He'd be pulling me against him, holding me so hard that I couldn't resist, letting his fingernails dig into me so I would push back against him and let his cock impale me even further. Then he'd start to move, pulling back as far as he could before thrusting hard into me, all the while telling me how much he loved fucking little sluts, feeling their cunts stretching around him as he filled them full of cock.

He'd be fucking me slow but hard, and squeezing whichever bits of me he could reach. Maybe he'd tell me to beg him to fuck me faster or tell him how much I liked being fucked and if I didn't comply quickly enough he'd slap my arse until I did what he said. After a while he'd stop with his cock as deep as possible inside me then he'd work the vibrator on my clit until he could feel me coming before thrusting into me some more. He'd tell me what a slut I must be to be coming like that when I'd been begging him to stop, and I'd be so hungry for more that I would scream my agreement.

After a while he'd turn me over and show me just how hard he can fuck me, slapping my arse while he rammed that fantastic cock deep into me, not letting me move except to push back against him, reaching under to grab and squeeze my tits or to rub my clit until I was completely helpless and could do nothing but come over and over again while he rode into me hard and fast and furious for as long as he could hold out before he came too and collapsed on top of me completely spent... well almost completely, he'd still have just enough energy to untie me and hold me and kiss me and let me know just how glad he was to be home.

Picket Fence
by Sommer Marsden

Nick found the Polaroid camera while we were doing our Spring cleaning. We had devoted our entire Sunday to lightening our household load. He waved it around with a grin. "Think they still make film for these things?"

I glanced up from a box stuffed full of knick knacks that I hadn't seen since I packed them. When we moved in, they went directly under the bed to be dealt with later. I wouldn't even unpack the box. The whole thing was going straight to charity.

"Actually, they do. I was at the pharmacy the other day and they had it hanging behind the counter. I guess enough people still have them that they continue to make film. Why?"

"Just curious," he said still grinning. Then he started holding up items from an old bag of clothes.

"Ditch it… ditch it… ditch it…" I sighed. "Put them all back in the bag and give the whole bag away."

"What if there's something good in here?" he joked, tying the bag closed.

"If we don't miss it, we don't need it. Time to get the clutter out of here. Then we can paint and redo the floor and actually have a home. Not a messy fixer-upper. A home."

Nick nodded and smiled. "Fine. But I'm keeping the camera."

"Keep the camera," I laughed. "I don't care."

Then I forgot about it.

Two days later he called me at work to tell me not to cook. He'd be picking up dinner. Fine by me. Any night I can eat without cooking is a fine night in my opinion.

When I got home, I poured myself a glass of wine and settled on the sofa, relishing the freedom from figuring out what was for dinner. He came through the door a few minutes later with a takeout bag in one hand and a small paper bag in the other.

"What's for dinner?" I asked, sipping my wine.

"Charlie's Bistro. We have roasted chicken, corn pudding, fresh bread and steamed green beans."

I loved Charlie's. The best take out around. There food was like mom's home cooking. Or in the case of my mom, better. "And?" I knew him too well.

"And just because I love you, half of a Sin Cake. I pointed to the one with the extra chocolate shavings on the top. Do I take care of you, or what?" Nick walked into the dining room and set the bag on the table. "Don't you want to know what's in the other bag?" he called.

"I hadn't even give the other bag a thought," I teased, following him. "Once you mentioned Sin Cake my brain short circuited."

I unpacked the bag from Charlie's and revelled in all the tasty smells. Nick shook the little paper bag at me. OK, I would play.

"A pregnancy test?" I said, reading the name on the bag. It was from the pharmacy up the street. "Are you pregnant?"

"Nope. Try again?"

"Condoms? That would be a waste of money, though, with me on the pill." I popped open the chicken container and then the containers of side dishes.

"Nope."

"I give up," I sighed. I was starving and ready to eat. No

more 'what's in the bag' game for me.

Nick tossed me the small bag and I barely caught it. I peeked inside and was instantly confused. "Film?"

"Polaroid film," Nick corrected, filling our plates with food.

"How very exciting for you," I laughed. "You bought film. For an ancient camera. Did you forget that we own a top of the line digital?"

"Of course not," he said softly and then handed me my plate. "But digital doesn't have the panache of the old Polaroids. All vibrant inside their little white borders."

"Ooh-kay. So what's it for?"

"I'm going to take your picture," he said.

As we sat and ate on the sofa and sipped our wine, he wouldn't say anything more. He was going to take my picture. No matter how much I bugged him he would only shake his head, smile and say, "later".

When later finally came, I was on my third glass of wine. I was feeling no pain and in a rather relaxed mood. No dinner dishes to do. Nothing to do but settle in for the night with my husband. My kind of evening. Nick came out with the camera and slid the large film clip into the slot. Then he looked at me and said, "Take your blouse off."

"What?!" That woke me up. My warm wine buzz flitted out of reach. I stared at him. Certainly he wasn't serious.

"You heard me, Noel. Take your blouse off."

"How much have you had to drink?" I laughed nervously. I felt very uncomfortable but way down deep, I noted, I was also feeling sort of... turned on.

"One glass of wine. That's it. Come on, babe. Play with me. Take your blouse off." He stood patiently. Waiting.

"Fine." I proceeded to unbutton each of the tiny white buttons on my silk blouse. I pulled it off and laid it on the sofa. My hands shook a little as I did it.

"Now the bra."

"Nick–"

"Just do it, babe."

I did. I unhooked my bra and pulled it off slowly, watching his face the whole time. His expression was a mix of excitement and intensity. I laid my lacy white bra on top of my proper white blouse and straightened my spine. My nipples were dusky hard peaks but I would not comment on that. It could be the temperature change. It did not mean I was aroused by this odd shift in evening routine.

"There." I said almost petulantly.

"Thank you," Nick said. This time he gave me a small, reassuring smile. "Now hold them in your hands. Hold those beautiful tits in those elegant hands."

A shiver ran through me and I obeyed. His words and requests were so strange, but also intoxicating. I hefted my breasts in my hands, letting my fingertips stray over my deep pink nipples. His commands and my capitulation serving to heighten the pleasurable sensation. Excitement coursed through me, shooting straight to my sex.

Nick made a small sound and raised the camera. The flash was blinding, the noise so loud after having grown used to the quiet ways of a digital camera. The photo ejected like a broad, square tongue. Nick pulled it out, set it on the side table and watched me. Just to torture him, I lifted my breast to my lips and sucked my own nipple.

His voice hoarse, he said, "Now the skirt, Noel."

I stood, unzipped the side zipper of my work skirt and let it fall. I stood there, suddenly sure of myself in my black panties, garter and hose. Another flash, another whine. The second photo shot out of the camera. He set it with the first and nodded. He didn't have to tell me. I unhooked the hose, rolled them down and placed them with my other clothes. Next the garter. I folded it in half slowly and then turned to add it to the pile.

Flash. Whine. A third picture had been taken.

"Nothing like that perfect ass in a nice pair of black, lace panties," my husband said.

When I turned he gave me another nod and I shucked the panties. Completely nude I stood before him. He took the fourth picture and then eyed me warily. He seemed a little unsure. What would he ask me to do now?

"Lay back on the sofa for me, baby. Spread your legs."

I did and the flash blinded me yet again. I wondered what the photo looked like. I could feel my cunt swollen and wet. How did it look? Rosy red with shades of pink? Did it look as engorged and slick as it felt? Did my arousal show up on film? Were there glistening slicks of my own fluid between my thighs? I sighed and without him asking, ran a finger along the seam of my cunt. I rubbed my fingertip along the hard knot of my clit and shuddered.

Flash. Whine. The fifth picture ejected with a triumphant sound.

I slid two of my fingers into my cunt and flexed them, pushing and probing. I stroked my G-spot and continued to stroke my clit. My pussy clenched around my fingers and I arched my back to stroke deeper. I heard Nick take the sixth picture and when the flash flickered I came, contorting on the sofa as spasm after spasm coursed through me.

Then he was on me. Discarding his work pants and shirt. His face dark and serious. He still held the camera and he set it on the back of the sofa as he pushed my legs up and settled the swollen head of his cock against my opening.

"You are beautiful. Gorgeous. Thank you," he was almost babbling as he thrust into me.

I was still feeling the effects of my first orgasm. My husband's swollen cock sliding into me, stretching and filling me was enough to make me hum my pleasure against his warm shoulder.

"My pleasure," I sighed and laughed.

Nick fucked me slowly at first. Drawing out almost all the way only to slide slowly back in to the root of his cock.

He pushed into me slowly but thrust high inside my cunt. I would come again, I could feel it already. Then he pulled half way out, propped on one arm and aimed the camera at our bodies where they joined.

"I want you to see this the way I see it," he murmured and then pressed the button. Without removing the photo he set the camera back down and began to fuck me in earnest.

His movements grew faster and jerkier. His breath tearing in and out of him loudly. I pushed up against him, after flashes going off behind my closed eyelids. In my mind's ear I could hear the camera capturing what I had done. When he stiffened against me and came with a groan, I came right along with him. My pussy sucking eagerly at what he had to give.

We laid there listening to the silence for a few minutes. No sounds but our breathing. When I could stand it any longer, I swatted him playfully on the shoulder.

"Enough of this. Let me see them!"

When I flipped through the stiff little photos, was both surprised and pleased. They were beautiful. Sexy. Raunchy in a classy sort of way. I handed them back. "Nick, my face isn't in any of them."

"I know." He opened the side table drawer and put the pictures inside.

"You don't like my face," I teased, but I was half serious. Not a single photo showed me above the neck.

"I love your face. Your face is beautiful, you know I think you are beautiful. All of you. Head, body, brain, soul." He smiled and kissed me.

"Then why?"

"There's a very good reason." That's all he would say.

The following day, I came home to another take out bag on the dining room table. The Archer. I smelled roast beef. I smiled and headed to the kitchen for a drink. I found Nick at the large kitchen window that overlooks our backyard.

Backyard is a stretch, really. It's more like a post card sized swatch of grass and a small concrete patio that has gate access to the wide alley that runs the length of our block. On the far side of the alley, the county had put up a tall picket fence to block off the small area of woods beyond. It looked like Nick was staring at the fence.

I poured a glass of wine and walked up, resting my head on his shoulder. "What are we looking at?"

"Them," Nick said. His eyes met mine for a second and I detected a tiny flicker of what looked like fear.

I looked out to see four men standing in the alley. They were spaced several feet apart, each gazing at a section of the fence. I saw tiny squares, so tiny from my vantage point, I couldn't make out what they were.

"And why are we looking at them looking at the fence. Or whatever's on the fence. *What is* on the fence?"

"You are on the fence," my husband said and wrapped his arm around my waist, pulling me close.

"What?" I yelled and stiffened under his arm. I tried to pull free of him but he pulled me closer and held me tight.

"Before you get all upset, just listen to me."

I was torn between punching him in the forehead and staring at the men who were in the alley gazing at my naked body… and me touching myself… and my husband fucking me!

"I don't think there's anything you could say to make me not want to kill you right now," I hissed.

"OK, then just watch them."

I turned my attention to the gathering below while I fumed. I wanted to march out and tear them all down and shoo away the perverts staring at me, but I knew that would give away that I was the object of their attention. So, I watched instead. The tallest man reached out and touched his fingertip to a photo. Just a fingertip. Then he withdrew it and stuck his hands in his pockets. I wondered if he was fondling himself through his pocket as I had seen men do.

A hot white spark of excitement rolled through my belly and my face burned with shame. Now who was the pervert?

"Watch him," Nick said, pointing to the small dark man closest to us. I watched fascinated as he first touched himself through his khakis, and then, to my surprise, unzipped his pants.

"He's…" I trailed off as he pulled his stiff cock from his pants and started to beat off. His hand a blur over the purplish flesh of his member. He stared straight ahead at whatever picture he was viewing and continued to stroke himself ferociously.

Fluid flooded into my panties and I shifted my stance, trying not to show exactly what this was doing to me. There was no way I would give Nick's betrayal any kind of approval.

"He's in his own little world," Nick sighed, running his hand over my bottom absent-mindedly. I shifted my footing again as his gentle touch added to what I was feeling inside. "He's locked there. Him, his dick, and you." Then he turned to me and touched my hair. "This is why your face isn't in there, Noel. I've wanted to… share you for a very long time. I didn't' know how. Then I figured this out."

"And?" I tried to keep my voice steady, angry. How dare he without asking me first? But his soft words and obvious sincerity loosened some of the tight anger in my chest.

"And their reaction is just like my reaction is when it comes to you. How it has *always* been when it comes to you." He turned his attention back to the men so I did the same. Just in time to see the man who was so oblivious to anything but my image come in long, ropey white streams. Nick sighed.

"And what's the reaction?" I asked. Fascinated, I watched his come coat his hand and drip, as if in slow motion, to the alley floor.

"You're like a drug. To me, being with you is as high as I can get. They're only feeling a small part of what I feel every day."

Forgetting my anger and my urge to hide my arousal, I slid up against him. I watched as another man, not as brave as the one who had just brought himself to orgasm, stroked his erection through his slacks. I pushed my hips against Nicks and quickly he got behind me. He yanked up my skirt and pushed down my panties. I heard his zipper and it only increased my need and urgency.

Then he thrust up into me, my upper body pinned against the thick glass of the window. I braced myself, face and breasts smashed against the cool, smooth surface. He fucked me fast, both of us watching out the window as my pilgrims stared and touched and stroked. Nick reached around and gave my engorged clit a few slippery strokes and I came so loud I sobbed on my own release.

He stayed in me, growing softer inside my body. We watched quietly, panting in the dimming light, as they filed off one by one. When Nick pulled his cock from me and smoothed my skirt back down over my hips, the final one walked off.

"Why didn't they take them?" I asked.

"I have no idea. Maybe they're afraid if they do, there wont' be any more." He stared at me and hesitantly asked, "Will there be any more?"

"Let's eat and we'll think about it."

Our next photo-shoot was in the basement. Nick had always wanted to tie me up and he asked rather shyly if he could. I agreed. The thought of more photos of a second pilgrimage of men to our back alley was enough to rev me up. The thought of being bound forced my pulse into a high, faltering gait.

"This is perfect," Nick said, running his fingers over the headboard of an antique bed.

The bed had been in my family for years but it wasn't my style. The brass scrollwork was oxidized and overly feminine for my taste. It had been propped on end against the basement wall since we moved in. I looked at it in a whole new light now. Standing on end it was taller than me. Maybe a little more than six feet tall. The intricate scrollwork was perfect for looping bonds through. I pressed my back up against it and put my wrists to either side of my head. Nick stared for a moment.

"Put them out to the sides more. That way I can capture your bound hands but not your face," he said softly. I did, spreading my arms like wings.

Nick bound one wrist with a bright paisley scarf. The other with a black scarf. The feel of the silk sliding against my skin, pressing the tops of my wrists to the cold brass worked a shiver through me. My nipples stood out from my own excitement and the chill of the basement.

"Spread your ankles wide," he muttered, bending down between my legs.

I wondered for a moment if a rush of fluid would escape my body when I did. I was growing wetter by the second. I spread my legs wide and watched him fasten first one ankle, then the other. I stared at my left ankle encased in yellow silk, my right bound with purple. When he raised his head and smiled, I smiled back. Then he lowered his face to my parted thighs and pushed his tongue warmly between my damp folds. I threw my head back and moaned. I was so worked up that one slow drag from his tongue sent the muscles in my belly galloping.

Nick inched closer on his knees and buried his face in my pussy. He licked and nudged and probed until I had inadvertently tested each and every bond with my restless movements. I hovered right on the edge of orgasm and my husband knew it. He knew my body like his own. He moved back on his knees and aimed the camera at my swollen cunt. The first image was captured.

I panted and pleaded for him to forget the photos and come back, but he moved around while I struggled and took pictures. When he had seven shiny photos lined up in a row he laughed.

"You were very good, Noel."

I was furious. Bound, aroused and very ready to come, he had made me wait. I pouted.

"Come on, don't be mad, I'm not done with you." Then he picked them up one by one and held them before my angry gaze.

My swollen red pussy, shining with moisture. It looked like an exotic flower. My lower belly taut as I thrashed, a blur of movement in the photo. My bound wrists straining in my bondage, hands tight little fists. My breasts, nipples stiff, swaying with my impatient movements. My feet on tip toe as I struggled, my ankles swathed in bright fabric, my calf muscles standing out proudly. A side angle of my ass and thigh. And my throat. Head tossed back, a bright rosy ring along my throat and collar bone from my anger and arousal.

When he put the last photo down I was panting. Breathless. I wanted him more than I could ever remember. He dropped back to his knees and drank from me. Softly this time. Slowly until I was one taut muscle from head to toe, straining as I came against the dusty brass.

When he fucked me, it was slow and sweet. The fact that I couldn't touch him but he could touch me pushed me head over heels into another bright white climax.

The next day, I left work early. I was that eager to get home and watch with Nick. I knew he was getting home before me and I knew he would go out and place the pictures along the Picket Fence.

He wasn't in the kitchen when I arrived, so I called out and he answered me from upstairs. I found him in our bedroom, kneeling on the chaise lounge under our largest window.

"Higher point of view?" I joked but joined him there,

kneeling next to him on the sage green fabric.

"Yes. And they are already here. You missed a guy. Reached out like he was going to take one and one of the men from last time chased him off. Four of the five are from last time."

I scanned the men, recognising the four he spoke of. The fifth was younger. Possibly mid-twenties. We watched for a few minutes. A furtive stroke from one man. A shift of feet and pants from another. The young man pulled out a cell phone and dialled. I felt Goosebumps rise up on my body.

"What do you think?" I asked.

"Don't know but remember, baby, your face is not in there. Unless they get you alone and naked, no one will ever know. And I always space them out evenly so you can't tell which house they came, if any." He stroked my lower back and I pushed myself against his warm hand.

Nick worked his hand over me. Pinched my nipples, ran his palm up the inside of my thigh as we watched them. My body was humming with excitement as I gazed at the men who had gathered to see me bound and naked. I was a voyeur to their voyeurism. After a few moments, a woman strolled down the alley. She went immediately to the young man and he directed her to the Polaroids. At first she looked angry, then flushed, then as if she were calming. When he turned and spoke to the other men, she stood at his side. He pointed to his watch, made some hand gestures and all the men left. They seemed reluctant but willing.

"I think he just told them when they could come back," Nick whispered.

"Why would he do that? And why would they listen?"

"A man understands another man's needs."

"What do you mean?" I was confused.

"Shhh. Just watch."

So I watched. I watched the young man walk his girl forward. I watched him look at each photo of me. I watched him stop in front of the one I could only assume was his

89

favourite.

"Your pussy," Nick told me. "All perfect and swollen and ready," he sighed, stroking the back of my thigh through my skirt.

I watched him push her face first against the fence, watched her pale forearms brace against the light wood. I watched him lift her little plaid skirt and push her pale pink panties to the side. And I watched him fuck her with almost animalistic movements as they both stared at a single picture. I watched her come and clutch at the fence. I watched his ass tense up and his jittering movements as he came inside her.

My face was hot and I peeled my own skirt off without being asked. I continued to watch out the window where he was now kneeling before her. Her slim back braced against the fence. My photo over the yellow halo of her hair. I watched him lick her clean and I watched her come again. I did all this with my hands braced on the windowsill and my ass in the air as Nick watched over my shoulder. As he rode me and stroked from the inside out. And when the young woman below came again and clutched her boyfriends black hair in her little fists, he smacked my ass really hard and drove into me.

I came with my breath fogging up the window and my knuckles white from clutching the sill. I came with my husband whispering my name like a prayer as he shot into me.

Over dinner, we held hands. After a glass of wine, we kissed. When we sat down on the sofa and I curled up around him, Nick turned to me and touched my face.

"I'm thinking Wednesdays," he said with a smile.

"Sounds good," I laughed.

"Wednesdays can be picture day," he said, running his hands along the undersides of my breasts. Cupping me there, his hands big and warm.

"And Thursdays can be the viewing day."

He laughed. "That is fine by me as long as it is fine by you."

I nodded. "It is. I don't know how it turned out that way, but it is. Nick?"

"Hmm?"

"Why do you think no one has taken them? Not a single one?"

"I have no idea, babe," he said with a little shrug. "I'm glad, cause I get to see what happens to them when they see you and then I still get to keep the pictures." He pulled me so I was laying in his lap. He stroked my hair and I made happy noises at the attention.

"What if they do?"

"It's OK. We can take more."

I smiled. I couldn't help it.

Change Of Life
by Cathryn Cooper

The benches in the sauna were wide. Mariana and Sharaz lay full stretch, their arms touching, their fingers entwined.

'Men let me down,' said Mariana. 'Firstly I was raped by my father's friend. My father wouldn't believe me and even said that I'd probably led him on. Tosh! He weighed a ton. Like a whale. Now who would want to make love with a whale? My second big disappointment was when I got involved with my mother's lover. I didn't know he was. We used to rent a villa he owned in Turkey. When my mother went outside to lie down on a sun bed, he used to take me upstairs and give me sweet drinks. I know now that those drinks were drugged. I had an inkling what had happened, but because my mother favoured him so much, I thought it was OK. I didn't realise she *knew* what was going on – not until she complained he was giving me more attention than he was giving her. I tried to tell her that he strapped me down, but she didn't believe me.

He made me so angry. One night after they'd been drinking heavily, they quarrelled and slept apart. I crept into his room and strapped him down with the ones he used on me. He didn't wake up, but I gagged him with one of his own socks just to make sure. I put on some rubber gloves and got some nettles from outside, tied them in a bunch and began to sweep them over his backside. I made a point of pushing them into his crack – I even managed to get a stinging leaf into his anus. He moaned but didn't wake up. Starbursts of rash broke out all over his bum. Oh, I so loved doing that. I untied him and took the sock from his mouth before leaving. In the morning he was in agony, scratching and moaning about his sore behind. I loved that. The more he did it, the more I enjoyed it. Strange that you can achieve an orgasm just from excitement; but that's what happened to me. Amazing don't you think?'

Sharaz giggled and snuggled closer to Mariana's breast. She closed her lips over it and shut her eyes, sucking on it like some over-sized baby.

Mariana moaned with pleasure. 'I'll always remember that night,' she said in a faraway voice, her eyes half closed as she enjoyed the pleasure Sharaz was giving her. 'I enjoyed that orgasm, and I also enjoyed leaving Ahmed scratching and hopping around like a cat on a hot tin roof. That night altered my life. From then on it suited me to subdue men rather than have sex with them or love them. I still feel they let me down badly – both my father and Ahmed. My father had shut his mind to my problems and favoured his friend. And Ahmed had abused me and undermined my mother's affinity with me. I never forgave men for that. I swore I would always want to be in control. That's why I married Jamie.'

'You didn't need to marry him.'

Mariana shrugged. 'He suited.'

'Will you stay with him for ever?'

'How long's for ever? Anyway, he's good in some ways. He doesn't make demands on me that I can't fulfil. He makes good money.'

'That's useful.'

'And he doesn't get in my way.'

Sharaz smiled then leaned closer and nuzzled her ear. 'That's good.'

Sharaz took hold of the ladle, dipped it into the bucket

93

and poured some over the coals. The coals sizzled. She kept back a little and drizzled it over Mariana's breasts.

'I'm thirsty,' she said, licking at the trickle hanging in a droplet from Mariana's nipple.

'Then drink,' said Mariana. She cupped her hand around Sharaz's dark head and pushed her onto her breast. At the same time Sharaz's fingers tickled at her newly shaved labia. Tingling sensations curled upwards into her groin. Like electricity, she thought. No! More like the sting of a nettle, though gentler and rampant with possibilities.

'You deserve something better,' said Sharaz, raising her head just long enough to speak before returning her lips to where she preferred them to be.

'I'm getting something better,' said Mariana with a secretive smile.

'And even better,' said Sharaz, her dark eyes gleaming with intent.

Again she reached for the ladle, dipped it into the water and trailed it over Mariana's belly and down between her legs.

Mariana arched her back. The mouth that sucked her was gentle and all knowing; only another woman could possibly know how best to arouse another.

This was their special place and she was loath to leave it. After all, what did she have at home? Four walls and... she let the reality slip away. Who cares what she had at home? Even when she got there, today's events would still be with her.

Just as she always did – as though nothing out of the ordinary had happened – Mariana parked her car in the drive, then went in through the back door. With a gentle thud and an accompany rattle, her keys and bag landed on the kitchen table.

She hummed as she went upstairs and undressed and she was still humming and thinking of Sharaz, her new lover, as the spray from the shower soaked her hair and her body. As she soaped herself with a moisturising gel, she took deep breaths and her body seemed somehow cleaner, smoother – newer – beneath her hands.

Sweet-smelling lather frothed over her breasts, dripped off her nipples, and ran over her belly. Warm fingers of water ran between her legs.

She stretched her arms above her head and let the water wash the soap away – just like Sharaz had cleansed the past and what she had been from her body.

Turning off the shower she shook the last drops of water from her fingers. All the time she hummed and smiled.

Dreamily, she wrapped the bulk of a white towel around herself and cuddled it to her as though it were a person surrounding her, holding her close.

Who was that fresh-faced, almost youthful person she saw in the mirror? Her skin was gleaming. Her nose was shiny. She wrinkled it, then laughed, tossed her head and headed for the stairs. She got herself a magazine from the drawing room and a drink from the kitchen. Then she sat herself in front of the television, picked up the remote control and flipped from one channel to another until she found a film that looked interesting.

Intermittently sipping her drink, she glanced from magazine to television. Neither held her attention for long. She couldn't get Sharaz out of her mind. They'd stroked and kissed each other stupid; they'd compared breasts and sat on the floor with their legs open admiring their reflections in a mirror. They'd decided to shave off their pubic hair, exfoliating each other's and applying cream and talcum powder. After that they'd eaten some fruit, but not until trying it for size in their newly shaved quims.

All in all, a very good night.

A mellowness came upon her. Smiling to herself, she let the magazine fall into her lap, then she folded her arms across her chest and cuddled herself.

Supper was unwanted, but tiredness was descending on her fast. She was eager to get to bed, keen to close her eyes. As she touched herself she would pretend they were not her hands but those of Sharaz.

Yawns forcibly increased in frequency and intensity. Bed and the possibility of dreams – half-truths of reality – beckoned.

She bounced from the sofa and turned off the television, the heating and the lights. She climbed the stairs, her eyes bright with excitement and looking forward to reliving the afternoon all over again.

Still lost in her spell, she used the bathroom, then in the bedroom she took off her white cotton bathrobe and followed the curves of her body with softly caressing fingers. Thrills of pleasure made her make sweet, soft sounds like a cat does when it dreams by a glowing fire.

Cautiously, as if determined to hold the dream, she pulled back the covers on the bed.

She paused and blinked as reality hit her. All hint of dreams and softness left her face. There before her eyes were her black satin pyjamas. Next to them was her husband's more dubious attire.

'Shit!'

Dreams of the delicious Sharaz were temporarily put to one side as she remembered where she had left Jamie. She sprang to where the wardrobe covered one wall and opened the middle door.

'Sorry,' she said, as the wriggling form of her bondage-crazed husband came into view. Silently, she watched him. How ridiculous, she thought. Then she shook her head and ran her fingers through her damp, tousled hair. 'You silly cow!' she said to herself. 'What are you saying sorry for? He can't bloody hear you!'

She reached for the buckles that strapped her husband's wrists together. Her fingers actually touched the cold metal and harsh leather but went no further. She hesitated. A questioning look came to her eyes. She frowned. Did she really want this man beside her in bed tonight as she dreamed of her new love, her new life?

Her hands retreated, and so too did her mind. Still frowning as she asked herself why this had ever started, she stepped back and regarded the man before her.

As he wriggled against his bonds, she covered her mouth with her hand, then moved it as she reminded herself that he could not hear her laughter, though of course, because she had touched the buckles, he would be aware of her presence.

What went on in his mind, she asked herself, when he was bound up like this? What went on when she was ordering him about or beating his bare backside? Sexual thoughts, yes, but what sort of sexual thoughts?

She began to laugh. There he was, a black leather hood covering his head, his wrists strapped together and bound above him. His ankles were fastened in a similar fashion and, to finish it all off, he wore a leather belt around his waist that had thinner straps coming off from it and diving between his legs. Another strap came from those two and divided around his scrotum and shaft.

Mariana's laugh got louder. Not that Jamie could hear or see. The mask covered his eyes and his ears. He was in a world of his own.

She began to rock backwards and forwards from the waist. Tears ran from her eyes and her shoulders shook with mirth. As she laughed, she tried to speak, but had difficulty doing so. At last it came out.

'You look bloody ridiculous!' she cried. She went on laughing. It only diminished when she at last took a good long look at her husband.

Suddenly she was seeing both him and herself anew. The laughter in her throat bubbled to a halt. She wiped at her damp eyes, then, as her last chuckle turned to a sneer, she shook her head and her expression was full of regret.

'What the hell am I doing with the likes of you?'

Not for the first time that day, the past came back to haunt her. Turkey and Ahmed came to her mind and her sneer changed again. A deep frown creased her brow. A scowl came to her mouth.

'Stuff you, Jamie! Stuff you all!'

Grabbing the wardrobe doors with both hands, she slammed them shut, turned her back and leaned against them.

'That,' she muttered with a powerful sigh, 'is that!'

As she rested her head against the wood, she heard the muffled wrigglings from within. Normally, Jamie would be in there for two to three hours. That was the time span he preferred. So far he had been in there for seven hours and would now be in there until the morning.

'My choice,' said Mariana with an air of finality. 'Not yours.'

With a final pat of the wardrobe door, Mariana went to bed. In the darkness of the wardrobe Jamie wriggled like a maggot on a hook.

La Cage Aux Folles
by Kaycie Wolfe

My name is Merril and I hate the fact I always have to spell it out. Older people, when introduced, mishear it as 'Beryl'. I took to enunciating the first syllable in an exaggerated manner but felt like a koi carp, and people were so taken with my facial contortions I'd still end up having to repeat it. It was my father's choice. I should have been a Jane, or a Linda; people know where they are with Janes and Lindas. I suppose people know where they are with me, once they get over the obstacle of my name, or they have until now.

'Good old Merril, always so accommodating,' friends and colleagues say to my face; reliable, but boring, they might as well add, I see it in their eyes. My name, the only thing about me deemed worthy of real interest.

'Oh, as in Streep?' strangers say, once they've cottoned on; and I smile, after all, she is something of a heroine of mine, before pointing out that hers has only one 'r' and a 'y'. Two years ago, on my fiftieth birthday, I toyed with the idea of changing my spelling to hers, so that when asked the question, I could simply smile and say, 'exactly!' Perhaps then some of her kudos would rub off, and I too, would become a woman of substance, a woman to be reckoned with. But I was put off by the thought of having to explain it to everyone. I think that was when the thought of running away first occurred.

Running away seems something men do rather than women. Certain middle-aged men, with families and mortgages around their necks, who one day, without warning, simply leave their desk at the Inland Revenue; close the door on their tidy semi, leave the people carrier in the garage, and walk right out of one existence to begin again from scratch, leaving no forwarding address. My first ever Relate client sixteen years ago was married to such a man. She was a Linda, and was utterly devastated, poor thing. It was a week before the first postcard arrived, bearing a Spanish postmark, saying simply, *Sorry – I'm all right*. A week later, another, saying, *Please don't worry about me. Love to the kids*; before the third and final instalment dropped onto the mat, *Just get on with your own life*.

It was the 'just' that upset her so much; as if it were that simple. I helped her voice her anger. I felt it too, what a cruel thing to do to someone. Whereas now, travelling alone on this train out of Waterloo, with no one but my solicitor knowing my destination, I feel a kindred spirit. And, for the first time in my life, feel truly free. Linda's husband of course, abandoned not only a spouse, but three dependent children, whereas ours...

Ours, why does that word bring me up short? Perhaps because through long years of marriage 'ours' had gradually given way to 'mine' and 'his'. Since the children moved away to forge their own lives, the house evolved into defined areas where Roger and I led increasingly parallel existences. Mine, the small sitting room-cum-study where I tend to my case-notes and read novels about lives more fascinating and fulfilling than my own. His, the large lounge with state of the art sound system and oversized TV for watching sport and the German porn channel he thinks I don't know about. The lawns and hedges are his; the flowerbeds, mine. Money is not an issue, as an only child I inherited well from my parents, and his job provides him a reasonable income and a new BMW every two years. My inheritance (there's that 'mine' again) burns no hole in my pocket, and I, being less ostentatious, am content with my little Fiesta.

The kitchen once also came under my sphere of influence, but, since the children left, he set about re-inventing himself as a foodie and increasingly laid claim to it. Last year, he went in for that Masterchef competition on TV. He was full of it. Told all our friends, spent a fortune on recipe books, recorded every programme, rehearsed every dish. He didn't win, but prided himself on getting through to the semi-final. It was his banana soufflé that let him down.

He arranged a dinner party the following weekend and cooked it again for both sets of neighbours to prove he could get it right. I do not care for banana. The truth is, I envied him, at fifty-five, he'd found something in life to get excited about. And, buoyed up by his newfound fame, it wasn't long before he found a new source of stimulation for a rather different appetite. Which reminds me, the living arrangements: once the children left home we opted for separate bedrooms. It was my idea, and given what was going on, or rather not going on, it seemed the best thing. Anyway, Roger did not object.

Roger. No one calls a child Roger any more. The only Roger you hear of nowadays is the one some stud gives his mistress; rather different to what Roger used to give me two or three times each month… that well choreographed stiff waltz that suddenly turns into a quickstep and always ends well before the music is finished. In earlier days, his fingers would carry on where his penis left off, but as time went by, he ceased bothering with the encore. When he was away on business and I had the house to myself, I'd sometimes dance alone, and allow my hands and fingers licence to roam. It sufficed.

Roger had always tolerated my Relate work rather than

101

shown any real interest in it. At parties, I'd overhear him damning me with faint praise.

'Oh yes, Merril's a dab hand at all that touchy feely stuff, whereas I'm just a practical kind of guy who brings home the bacon and enjoys the simple pleasures of life.'

Which was my cue to cut in, smile, and say, 'Not so simple, surely darling?'

A limited, but fair, exchange, which rather summed up our marriage, until Masterchef.

It was a few months after Masterchef that Relate were seeking another counsellor to train as a sex therapist at my local office. My supervisor seemed surprised when I mentioned I was thinking of applying.

'After all these years, why now?' she asked.

I said it seemed like a good idea, and was immediately aware how lame that sounded. She said I'd better come up with a more telling answer at the interview. I didn't dare tell her I was competing with Roger.

It was not that I lacked interest in sex, far from it. It's just that apart from some early adolescent fumbling with a female classmate and a boy in sixth form who later turned out to be gay, my hands-on experience had been limited to Roger, and what Ben Elton quaintly called the pleasures of the palm. With Roger, the action and the feelings never quite got in step.

However, my counselling work at Relate provided a measure of excitement, allowing me to gaze through net curtains and peer under the duvets into intimate corners of people's lives. I would eagerly explore my clients' sexual lives, but with more interest in meanings than mechanics. What does it mean to this woman, to feel her husband's penis inside her; or to this man, to offer that part of himself to her? What message does this hand bear, as it snakes across the silent reaches of the marital bed? And what is this breast saying, as it tenses under his touch? I'm skilled at helping couples find language for such ritual thrusts and

102

fumbling, and even if Roger and I never spoke to each other like that, the loss was ours alone, and at least I could take comfort in my ability to enable others to relate at a deeper and more rewarding level.

I suppose, if I'm honest, there was always a part of me that wondered about what I might be missing; perhaps that's why, before it was too late, I put my name forward to train as a sex therapist. It seemed safer than an affair.

In the days prior to the interview, I devoured the course prospectus and a weighty tome called *Understanding Sexual Dysfunction* I found on the counsellors' bookshelf at Relate. It's not that I was shocked, or embarrassed, by photographs of vulvas and penises in various states of arousal; it was the text that put me off; the starched white-coated language of clinical gravitas. It might prove interesting to analyse humour but it's hardly very funny; something similar can be said of sex. Here was sex reduced to a complex system of neurotransmitters, plumbing, and hydraulics, culminating in a four-stage model of *Desire, Excitement, Orgasm, Resolution,* which has more to do with mechanics than with persons, meanings and feelings.

I tried explaining as much at the interview, but sensed that my examiner thought me a prude. Was I perhaps, 'a little too buttoned-up' she asked, to put clients at sufficient ease to discuss their orgasms, erections and ejaculations, whether premature or retarded? She then stared hard, presumably to ascertain whether I understood the latter term, or defying me to shatter the image she had of me. I considered demonstrating my knowledge, and whether or not to allow the odd 'cock' or 'cunt' to slip from my lips in order to prove that I, too, was at ease with my sexuality, but didn't like her enough to indulge in those kind of games. So, I just smiled.

When I informed Roger of her decision, he expressed a level teaspoon of disappointment before retreating into his recipe for Magret de Canard au Poivre Vert with

Dauphinoise potatoes. I think he was rather relieved.

It was at the Relate Christmas party that it must have started. Jas (short for Jasmyne, I gather) had not long moved into the area. I'd met her only a couple of times at our fortnightly case discussion group. On the first occasion, she showed particular interest in a case I was presenting in the group. My client was Harry, a slight, rather attractive, young GP, whose partner had come home early from work to find him wearing her underwear, lipstick and squeezed into her lycra mini-dress.

She had accompanied him to Relate merely to state in front of a witness that their relationship was over. 'I only hope you can do something with him,' was her parting shot to me, as she slammed the door. Poor Harry looked across at me, mournfully. I saw him for seven sessions after that, during which we explored the origins and meanings of his cross-dressing and what, if anything, he wished to do about it. Shame always shrinks from the light of day, and I told the group I was impressed by the trust Harry had shown in me. At which point, Jas interrupted, saying she thought I should look more closely at what I might represent for Harry.

'How do you mean?' I asked.

'Well, I wonder how he sees *you,* Mary?'

'Merril. My name's Merril.'

'Oh, well Merril, you're clearly considerably older than Harry, perhaps he sees you as, a sort of, mumsy confessor?'

Mumsy. Hmm. I smiled.

Actually, I think Harry rather adores me. He certainly seems to admire the way I dress for counselling: usually trousers or a dark suit, skirt just below the knee, crisp shirt or top, all appropriate to role, age and figure (12/14). I wear little jewellery, but quality, and always understated. At the start of each session Harry always comments thoughtfully on my appearance; something Roger only ever does after someone else's observation prompts him to do so. Harry

104

liked my new skirt and even noticed it was cut on the bias! He said it went well with my new kitten-heel shoes.

'Aren't you being a little naïve, Merril? You'll be going shopping with him next.'

Jas's final comment pricked the atmosphere like a dart just as the facilitator was attempting to move us on to another member's case. She was right. I may indeed have been naïve about Harry, but not about her.

I was alive to Jas before she even opened her mouth. I knew she and I wouldn't get on; I didn't take to her physically. Her hair is cut in that short funky style that is probably called bed-head or wash-and-go, and always looks good, but on me would just look a mess. She dresses casually, more casually than I'd like if I had to suffer her picking through the entrails of *my* marriage. Hipster jeans, see-thru voile shirt worn over clingy white vest, pretty tasselled scarf thrown loose about her neck, low-slung belt, its large buckle drawing the eyes to her crotch, long painted nails that clearly don't suffer housework or gardening.

What her female clients make of her as their husbands eye her up and down, I dread to think. She clearly wants to look younger than her years, which I take to be mid-forties, but that slender frame somehow lets her get away with it. She reminds me of Trinny or Susannah on TV, whichever is the tall thin one with no tits but you still can't take your eyes off her.

And neither could Roger, at the Relate Christmas party, where he spent most of the evening telling Jas all about the 'Masterchef experience' and what a truly sensual and artistic activity cooking is, and how we all need to educate our children to appreciate and revere it the way the French and Italians do as a matter of course. Apparently, she and her husband have a second home in Tuscany, and she 'adores' the Italian way of life. In fact, her husband runs a property development business over there and is across in Italy for weeks at a time.

The signs are always there, if you look for them: a husband's more rigorous attention to shaving, the newly purchased soft-touch shirts and boxer shorts, late evenings at the office, and the sudden overnight meeting down in Bristol. That was the night I cracked the password for his computer: *masterchef1*, easy.

So Roger, your SENT email box states that our marriage is 'a sham', that in bed, I've been 'like a fridge', and you've come to see that your life with me has been like 'living in a cage' and it took 'just one kiss' from her 'luscious lips' to teach the caged bird how to sing!'

And Jas, such fulsome ejaculations by reply: so you l-o-n-g for him. Long to feel my husband's 'sweet kisses all down your spine, and beyond!' You lie awake, 'dreaming of a whole night together' when he's meant to be down in Bristol. In case discussion group, you almost feel sorry for the 'old sack' sitting opposite, as your labia 'glisten at the memory' of her husband's cock sliding up and down between your (little) breasts. How encouraging, Roger, for you to read of the 'electric thrill' at the Relate Christmas party, as your fingers brushed past her nipple as you reached for her glass, and how glad she was that she'd decided not to wear a bra. And to be told how welcome your cock feels inside Jas's 'warm, flowing cunt,' as she sits astride you. How uplifting, Roger, to be informed by such a woman that you were not born to live a caged, half-life.

Roger's company appeared to be taking off in Europe, judging by the number of meetings he was now required to attend in Brussels and Paris. He was away overnight at least a dozen times over the next three months, while I held the fort at home. At Relate, I continued to tend to my clients, and revealed no sign of chagrin at being rejected for sex therapy training in favour of Jas, who delighted in telling me how well she and the interviewer had got on and how much she was enjoying the early parts of the training. I simply smiled.

The shopping expedition with Harry was a great success. I took him to Monsoon where I helped him choose a rather fetching dress, and M&S, where I helped him select a skirt, two tops, a pair of 'Shapewear' knickers, some leggings, hold-up stockings and tights, as well as a pretty silk camisole that I rather wish I'd bought for myself. In return, Harry handed me an envelope containing a super-strength sleeping draft, which he said I should dilute in a sweet milky drink, sometime during the evening after which I should on no account drive or operate machinery. I thanked him and before going our separate ways, he promised to take some self-photos to show me at our next session. I smiled, knowing full well there would be no next session, at least not at Relate.

The Internet holds no truck with boundaries of class, gender, or attire. Anyone can go anywhere, and via links through Google and Wikipedia, I was soon gazing upon vivid testimonies to man's ingenuity and the triumphs of mechanics and engineering. I spent an enthralling hour perusing various items with names such as 'Houdini', 'Stallion', and the more prosaic 'CB2000/3000', along with several user reviews. These all came under the heading of male chastity devices, and usually consist of two main sections: a leather, metal or plastic cage for the penis, attached to a heavy-duty ring for the balls, the whole ensemble secured by a steel padlock. The more substantial versions are made of chrome, sometimes plastic coated in a range of colours. These devices are claimed to render intercourse impossible and masturbation/erections if not entirely preventable, then certainly extremely uncomfortable. I was sorely tempted by one called 'The Curve', its clear, polycarbon downward-curving tube fully enclosed the placid penis, and several photographs of it in situ I found extremely appealing. However, I rejected this in favour of an earlier model, the CB 2000, for the sole reason that its use of a series of bars, rather than the one-piece tube gave a more authentic cage-like appearance. This, along with its tamper-proof qualities, steel padlock and two keys, made it seem a bargain at £79.99 inc p&p, and I readily placed my order online. I was in buoyant mood as I lay back enjoying a leisurely candlelit bath and contemplated my purchase. Over the next few days as I awaited delivery, I found myself humming under my breath, lines from an old pop song lodged somewhere in the far reaches of my mind, 'You can look but you better not touch!'

Roger was at work the day the parcel arrived. Before opening it, I had the brainwave of heading straight out to WH Smith where I bought a large pack of Plasticine and, back at home, set about sculpting a set of male genitalia on the kitchen table. It was most absorbing, being able to give the penis any girth or length I wished, and I set it at various provocative angles. Eventually, I stopped giggling and gave serious thought to my fading memories of Roger's equipment in its un-aroused state. Circumcised, with a pronounced bell-shaped head, his member hangs slightly to the left, as seen from his perspective, and his balls hang low, and seem of average size; nothing to compare it with really, other than the Relate books and a few Internet images. At last, my sculpture was complete and I set about fitting the CB2000 to the model. I found it awkward, and it took some time before I finally snapped the steel padlock securing the cage's somewhat squashed and mangled contents. Showing great patience, I repeated the entire procedure several times until I was confident I knew what I was doing and had no need to keep checking the written instructions. After all, I could expect no assistance from the wearer. As I put it away, I re-read the accompanying blurb, which suggested that many men find an exquisite satisfaction in being restricted in this manner, and their dependence upon the key-holder's benevolence to release their pent up sexual urges. I found this intriguing, but disturbing, as I had no intention of adding one iota to the ecstasy Roger and Jas found in each other's bodies; quite the reverse. I read again every one of their desire-drenched emails, which served to reassure me as to the unlikely possibility of such an outcome. I printed off the emails, sent copies to my solicitor with a covering letter regarding my intention to commence divorce proceedings, and settled down to await Roger's return.

Administering the sleeping draft proved something of an obstacle. Roger is not used to me making him a bedtime drink and at first declined the mug of hot chocolate, but on catching a whiff of mine, he changed his mind and succumbed. It was one o'clock when I crept into his room. I waited some moments before switching on the bedside light. He never flinched. His mobile lay on the bedside table, still switched on. It showed a text message from Jas... *Goodnight my eagle, not long until you soar again in my arms, xx.* I switched it off.

It was a long time since I'd gazed at my husband's genitals, and never so freely. I find it quite magical, how something so soft and puny can be readily transformed into poker-firm maleness; the way the balls swell and draw up tight inside the corrugating sack, and all brought about by the mere thought, look, or touch of a woman.

I studied the bell-shaped helmet, with its pronounced coronal ridge and tiny mouth, its lips closed like a small child's in sleep. Gently, I lifted the flaccid penis, exposing the ball sack, in its innocent slumber. 'The sack,' that's what your bitch called me, isn't it darling?' I whispered, 'Well, let's make a new nest for Jas's precious little eagle...'

My earlier practice session served me well, it needed to, for my fingers trembled with excitement as I enclosed my husband's cock-bird in its bright new cage and secured it firmly to the ball ring with the locking pins provided. When at last my fingers snapped the steel padlock shut, my breast swelled on a tide of newfound power. I took a long hard look, and was pleasantly surprised at the sheer beauty of my husband's cock so caged. I fetched my digital camera and took photographs from every possible angle, including several close-ups. I leaned forward, planted a delicate kiss on the bars of the cage, and knew that for the first time in my life, I had found true freedom. I put back the duvet, crept from the room, gathered my suitcases and called a taxi.

En route to the station, an inane grin kept breaking out at the thought of Roger waking to find his manhood encaged. I imagined him rushing to the garage, attacking it with pliers and screwdriver, but put my faith in the manufacturer's boast that it would require a locksmith, or the key-holder, to set the caged bird free.

As Eurostar emerged from the tunnel into the bright light of a new French morning, I knew that in caging Roger I had discovered my destiny. I would spend the next three months planning my transformation from good old Merril, into Mistress Meryl, a woman who understands the benefits of knowing how to take complete charge of a man.

The silver-haired gentleman in the seat opposite must have noticed my fingers toying suggestively with the bright shiny key suspended from my neck on a thin silver chain, and nestling just above the first hint of cleavage. Slowly, he lowered his copy of the Financial Times; his quizzical stare met mine. And I smiled.

Travel Broadens The Mind
by Kirsten Schubinski

I'm not sure how long I've been here, in this room, in the dark. They blindfolded me before I got here, whoever they are, and every now and again the door of my cell opens and someone, a man, brings me food. I can tell it's a man by his smell. Sweaty, dirty, with a spicy enigmatic overtone which I can't place. I think I may have been here two weeks but it's difficult to tell; shock does strange things to you. I sleep a lot and devour the food they give me. I seem to be really hungry. The man who brings me the food often lingers in the cell, watching me eat before closing the door and walking away. It used to put me off but now I've got used to it – it's as if he's never seen a woman eating before. And a blindfolded one at that. I miss a lot of food and it slips down my chin and sometimes between mouthfuls I can hear him breathing. But he hasn't touched or harmed me in any way and I'm too damn hungry and disorientated to feel self-conscious.

We'd been warned about rebels and kidnappings in the area but I guess I never took it seriously. Neither had any of the other businessmen on the bus, talking into their mobile phones and laughing loudly together. I was one of only two women on the bus and halfway through my round the world trip, savouring the fact that now I really was getting away from the demands and responsibilities of civilisation.

Suddenly I'd realised that our bus had stopped and yet there was no checkpoint or settlement in sight. Then I heard shouting outside and gunshots. The next thing I know loads of armed men are on the bus, pointing their rifles at us, and shouting at us to get off. There are about twenty of them, all with the slanty, almost oriental, eyes of the region, high cheekbones and the kind of tan only acquired through years of hard living high up in the mountains. They wore the traditional long smocks over trousers or jeans, I remember, and chains of bullets were slung round their necks. Once outside, they had got us up against the wall of the bus and frisked us for our valuables. Then they kicked the back of our knees and pinned us to the ground before blindfolding us. I felt myself being picked up and thrown into the back of some kind of jeep, along with two other hostages. The jeep carried us, bruised and sick, up hills and down mountains, on a journey which seemed to take for ever, until we arrived here – wherever here is.

I don't know what has happened to the others. They're businessmen so I suppose their firms will pay a good sum of money for their return. But me, what am I worth? I'm not sure why they are still keeping me here. For a while I was terrified they would try to molest or rape me but thankfully that doesn't seem to be part of their agenda. Now I exist in a kind of limbo; sleeping, dreaming, waking to the sound of footsteps outside my door, eating then sleeping again, being led to the hole in the ground which is the toilet and squatting in front of this mysterious man, my jailer.

Hearing the sound of his footsteps approach my cell door has become the highlight of my day. Like a clock, his regular visits give me some idea of time passing, of morning, afternoon and evening. I sit and wait for those footsteps to come and try to guess what he looks like. Pat, pat, pat down the hall come those slippered footsteps. Then the sound of the key in the lock, a creak as the door opens. A pause as he crosses the room towards me and that familiar smell again. I hated it in the beginning, but now it intrigues me, as I wonder what spices it is made up of and try to guess how old the man might be. I hold my breath as he leans over me and something rough and slightly damp brushes my lips. His hair. Maybe it's my imagination, but this time he seems to linger over me after putting the plate down and I freeze, sniffing the air. His scent is even stronger now and I can feel the warmth of his body. Suddenly dry fingertips are at my neck, and I gasp, but don't cry out. Somehow I don't think they'd like it if I scream.

My breath is coming very fast as I wait to see if he is about to strangle me. His hands remain tight around my throat, but the pressure does not increase. My logic kicks in and I desperately reassure myself that if they were about to kill me they would not bring me food first.

And then suddenly for some reason I know he is not about to murder me and I relax a little, wondering what is coming next. His hands are tight and strong on my throat, but not uncomfortable. Slowly he brings them down, down my neck until he reaches my collarbone and then down into my shirt, pulling it open by separating his hands.

I'm not wearing any bra and my breasts fall out of my now gaping shirt, into the cool air. I hold my breath, waiting. He is still very close, but doesn't touch me. A moment later I hear him move back and away from me and settle down a little distance away. I can just about hear his breathing. The minutes pass like hours while he just sits there. I get a vision of what this must look like – I'm sitting here in this tiny room, blindfolded, my tits hanging out, while some strange terrorist sits and just looks at me. I should be terrified but I'm not, I realise – I'm aroused.

I am very aware of the slight weight of my breasts, I can feel the cool air touching them and I sense the nipples harden and swell. Maybe it's my imagination but I think his breathing is faster than before. Still nothing happens.

113

After a while I think I may as well eat the food he's brought me and I fumble around for the plate. Suddenly he moves quickly towards me and his hand brushes mine as I fumble for the plate in the dark. He snatches it away from me and a minute later I feel his dry fingers again, this time at my lips. He separates them with his hand, opens my mouth wide and starts feeding me with the other hand. Part of me is in shock, but the other part of me is hungry and enjoying the game. Another part wonders if he is into rape after all.

Sometimes pieces of food miss my mouth and slip down my chin, onto my breasts. I can feel the slimy pieces of food sliding down my chest and I want him to move them away. I want him to touch me. The more he feeds me, ignoring my exposed breasts, the more my nipples harden and lengthen, trying to cover the distance between us. The food is all gone and we sit there motionless, until I move ever so slightly towards him, wanting his dry hands again. But he pushes me back, and I let out a tiny moan, despite myself. He laughs, a soft chuckle, and then we listen to each other's rapid breathing in the tiny room.

Suddenly I feel warm breath on my left nipple and his other hand ever so gently circling my right. His tongue is applying such slight pressure I'm not sure it is really his tongue, until he starts to suck at me, slowly, gently, deliberately. At the same time he pulls at my other nipple, again at the same rhythm, softly and gently pulling my breasts towards him and back again. I moan again, loudly, as I feel him begin to suck and pull at me a little harder. He moans too, and the sound shocks me, it is so deep and hoarse and turned-on.

My arms grab at him, and I touch his neck, his head, his hair, his mouth. I give him my open mouth and then my tongue. Our tongues meet briefly, gently, then his tongue begins to explore my mouth, first licking my lips softly then flicking in and out of the sides, then probing my mouth

114

more deeply, sucking on me, softly biting my lips. I can hear him panting.

But now he's kissing me too greedily, too quickly. His rough cheeks are stinging my face, his mouth bruising me. After a minute more of discomfort I turn my head away. A pause, then I feel him take my chin in one hand and turn me back to face him. He takes my upper lip between his teeth. I can feel his sharp incisors biting down, oh so gently, on the flesh. Then he kisses me, unbelievably gently, for what seems like an age, until I have absolutely no resistance left. I feel light as air and as weak as paper.

All this time he has been pulling and pushing at my breasts, building up my sexual tension, until I feel my clitoris pushing at my jeans. I want him inside me, whoever he is, my invisible lover-come-jailer. I don't suppose he's heard of the sexual revolution, I know for a fact that he doesn't wash very often, but I'm sure he knows how to fuck.

Anyone who knows how to touch and kiss a woman like this will know how to fuck her just the way she needs to be fucked. I reach out for his cock but his clothes get in the way and he chuckles again. I arch my back and let out a soft scream as he bites at my nipples and takes my body in his arms. Then he bites my neck and I let go, willing him to do whatever he wants with me. For a moment we stay in this position. Then he gently pushes me back against the wall, disengages himself and his soft footsteps leave the room. The door bangs behind him and he is gone.

After Hours
by Kristina Wright

Dinner in the city hadn't been what Natalie had in mind after a hectic day at the hospital, but now that she was sitting across from Ryan, enjoying a wonderful meal at one of the best restaurants in the city, she couldn't help but smile.

'I'm really glad you talked me into going out tonight,' she said. 'I would have been happy to stay in and curl up with you, but this is nice.'

Ryan's dark eyes sparkled in the candlelight. 'Wait until later.'

'What happens later?'

'You'll have to wait and see.' He reached across the table and stroked the inside of her wrist. 'What are you wearing under your skirt?'

'You'll find out later,' she answered, a little shiver dancing up her spine. She wasn't wearing anything at all under her short, black skirt, but she wanted to tease him the way he was teasing her.

'I can't wait. I want to be so deep inside you.'

She shifted in her chair; suddenly, instantly aroused by Ryan's intense gaze. The sexual tension was nearly palpable. 'Oh God, you're making me crazy.'

Ryan laughed. 'I'm making us both crazy. Let's get out of here.'

After the check had been paid, Ryan led Natalie in the opposite direction from where he'd parked the car. She assumed this was part of his plan for the evening and contentedly tucked her arm through his and pressed her face to his shoulder. She felt like a cat in heat, wanting to rub her body all over him until he fucked her silly. She giggled, feeling a little drunk. Whether it was from the two bottles of wine they had shared at dinner or the sexual anticipation, she wasn't sure. Nor did she care.

When she realised they were outside the building where he worked, she paused. 'Why are we here?'

Ryan led her through the door and into the lobby. 'I forgot some paperwork I need for tomorrow. It'll only take a second.'

The security guard wasn't too happy about them going up to Ryan's office after hours, but Ryan finally convinced him it would be all right. Once the doors closed behind them on the elevator, Ryan pulled Natalie close and kissed her. She melted against him, his solid erection letting her know how aroused he already was.

He kept kissing her as the elevator climbed to his office floor. Finally, the doors opened and he pulled back. 'We're here.'

Natalie blinked at him. 'You'd better hurry up, because I don't know how much longer I can wait before I rip your clothes off.'

He laughed. 'You're cute when you're feeling slutty.'

He took her by the hand and pulled her into his dark office, closing the door firmly behind him.

'Ryan, what are you doing?'

He pulled her close, fondling one breast until the nipple hardened beneath her silk blouse. 'What do you want me to do?'

She looked at the door, expecting a security guard to burst in on them at any moment. 'I don't know if this is a good idea.'

'No?'

'No,' she said. She was having a hard time concentrating on what it was she was so worried about because Ryan was slowly pulling up her skirt.

He walked her backward until she was leaning up against the desk. Then he pressed against her, letting her feel the full, hard length of his cock. She moaned into his mouth as he kissed her, rubbing against him, desperate to feel him inside her.

'I know you've been having a rough week,' he murmured as he kissed and nibbled his way down her neck to her collarbone. 'So I thought I'd help you relieve your stress.'

Natalie ran her hands down his back, giving his ass a squeeze. 'How are you going to do that?'

'I'm going to fuck you on my desk.'

She moaned. 'You're bad.'

Ryan made as if to pull away. 'Well, we can go back to your place if you want…'

'Come back here,' she said, pulling him to her by his shirt. 'I want you to fuck me on your desk. Hard.'

'Oh, I will,' he promised. 'But I want to see what I'm doing.'

Ryan crossed to the wall and turned on the light. Natalie blinked in the suddenly well-lit office. The blinds were open and though they were twenty floors up and surrounded by empty office buildings, she felt exposed and vulnerable. Before she could change her mind about their naughty adventure, Ryan returned and took her in his arms.

'Relax,' he whispered as he lifted her up and sat her on the edge of the desk. 'Let me take care of you.'

Natalie braced her arms on the desk and spread her legs wider as he slid his hands up the insides of her thighs under her skirt. She shivered when his fingertips brushed her bare pussy.

'You're not wearing underwear,' Ryan said, his voice

husky with barely controlled lust. 'Naughty girl.'

Natalie giggled. 'What are you going to do about it?'

He knelt down in front of her and flipped the edge of her skirt up, baring her to his gaze. Then he kissed the inside of her thigh, following the same path as his fingers, until his tongue swirled around her engorged clitoris.

'Oh, Ryan,' she moaned, as she clutched at his shoulders. 'Lick me, make me come.'

It was so wrong, being here like this, but she didn't care any more. All she cared about was the feeling of Ryan's tongue on her cunt. Ryan slid a finger inside her as he licked her, making her gasp and thrash on the desk. She wanted more, wanted him inside her, wanted to come so badly she was gasping and whimpering with need.

After what felt like an eternity of licking and teasing, Ryan used his fingers and tongue to drive her over the edge to a delicious, powerful orgasm. Even though she knew they might get caught, she couldn't help moaning loudly from the intensity of her orgasm. As the spasms inside her body subsided, she sat up and smiled. 'That was incredible. Your turn,' she said.

Before he could respond, she was on her knees in front of him, unzipping his pants and freeing his hard cock. She moaned softly as she took him between her lips, sucking the head gently before taking more of him into her mouth. She looked up at him as she sucked, knowing he loved to look into her eyes while she held him in her mouth.

Ryan ran his fingers through her long hair, staring down at her. 'That feels so good,' he whispered.

She licked and sucked him, taking as much of him into her mouth as she could before slowly pulling back. All the while, she kept looking up at him, meeting his steady, intense gaze.

Ryan groaned and pulled away. 'I need to fuck you,' he said. He pulled her to her feet and kissed her. 'Turn around.'

119

Natalie turned so that she was facing the desk. 'Like this?' she asked, bracing her hands on the desk and wiggling her behind.

'Lower,' he said, putting his hand in the small of her back. 'I want your ass up so that I can admire it.'

She lowered her upper body until it was pressed against the desk. In this position, her high heels put her waist higher than the desk so that her ass was now sticking up in the air. Ryan pushed her skirt up over her hips, baring her from the waist down. It felt so naughty, being spread out like this on his desk. She shivered in arousal.

She heard rustling behind her and tried to see what Ryan was doing. Before she could ask, he came around the other side of the desk. She lifted her head to see him looping a length of nylon rope around her wrist.

'Where did that come from?' she said, hearing the excitement in her own voice.

'I've been saving it for a special occasion.' He knotted the rope around her wrist, then pulled her wrists together and bound them together. 'I'm going to tie you down so you can't get away.'

Part of her wanted to protest that this was crazy and too risky. But part of her, the part that was so turned on she couldn't stand still, wanted to be tied down and fucked. 'Oh really?'

Ryan moved around behind her again. 'Really. Now be a good girl and stop squirming.'

She obeyed, wondering what he was up to. The rope on her wrists tightened, then she felt him tying first one ankle, then the other, to the desk. She realised he had passed the rope from her wrists under the desk. Now she was tied to the desk, connected by her wrists and ankles and utterly helpless.

'Beautiful,' he murmured. His hands caressed her bare ass and up the insides of her damp thighs. 'What do you want, baby?'

She trembled under his gentle touch. 'You know what I want.'

'Tell me,' he said, slapping her ass hard enough to make her yelp. 'Tell me what you want.'

She could feel him behind her, the shaft of his cock pressing against her ass. Her legs were spread wide, she was completely exposed, and all she wanted was to feel him inside her. Now.

'Fuck me,' she whispered. 'Fuck me, Ryan.'

'Say please.'

She gasped as he slapped her again. 'Please,' she said. 'Please, please fuck me.'

The last word trailed off in a moan as he slowly slid inside her tight, wet cunt. He pulled back, then pushed deep inside her again. Over and over, in a steadily quickening rhythm, Ryan fucked her.

'Do you like this?' he asked. 'Do you like getting fucked on my desk?'

Natalie moaned loudly, straining at the ropes that bound her wrists. 'Yes, oh God, oh yes!'

She gripped the edge of the desk with her bound hands, using what little leverage she had to meet his thrusts. He felt so good, so hard, inside her. She had never been so turned on as she was in that moment, tied to the desk while Ryan fucked her from behind. The edge of the desk rubbed against her clit on every downward stroke of his cock and she dug her nails into the wood, aching to come again.

'Fuck me. Fuck me, Ryan. I'm going to come again,' she gasped.

He gripped her hips tightly, thrusting harder into her so that every motion drove her aroused clit against the desk. 'Come for me,' he demanded. 'I want you to feel you come on my cock.'

She pushed her ass against him as hard as she could, every muscle straining in her need for release. Being tied down, nearly immobile, only served to heighten her arousal as Ryan controlled the speed, the depth, the force of every stroke of his cock inside her. She wanted more, harder, deeper, and she begged him in a voice that bordered on hysteria, her need to come was so great.

She moaned and gasped as his cock glided along her G-spot and bumped her cervix in that pain-to-pleasure feeling she loved so much. He fucked her hard, the way she begged him, driving her higher and higher until she couldn't take it any more. Finally, finally, she came, screaming his name, her body rigid and straining against her bonds. Her cunt clamped down on his cock, rippling along the length of him, and his answering groan let her know he was coming with her, deep inside her.

They lay there for a long time, Ryan draped over her limp body as her orgasm subsided.

He pushed her hair off her neck and kissed her damp skin. 'You are incredible, love.'

'Mmm, thanks,' she murmured. She was drained, sore and exhausted, but it was the good kind of exhaustion that would leave her smiling in the morning. 'You really know how to make a girl forget about work, but how am I going to hide these rope burns tomorrow?'

'Call in sick and I'll take care of you.'

Natalie could only imagine what that might entail – and she liked it. 'Don't forget to bring the rope.'

In The Saddle
by Primula Bond

I nearly reversed out and drove away again. I hate country weekends at the best of times. All that walking, all that jollity, all that mud. Charades, butlers, and which fork do you use? But I especially hate them when I barely know the host, let alone the other guests. So why the hell was I two hours away from my comfort zone because some guy with brown eyes caught me in a devil-may-care mood the other night and invited me to stay?

You always get lost in the country, too. And that wet, windy Saturday afternoon I was lost. Or so I thought, till I found the big wrought-iron gates. The long drive between elegant trees. So this was no weekend cottage. This was a fucking baronial pile. Thing was, after the gates and the long drive, I still couldn't find it.

I nosed the car down a promising fork where the gravel was less pitted and studied the cocktail menu where he'd scribbled his number. Tried to phone it. Oh, and the countryside has no signal.

At last I bumped through a kind of crumbling stone archway dripping with ivy, and there I was in the middle of a spotless stable yard. The house, and the guy, and all his braying friends, must be nearby.

The rain had stopped for a moment. Two listless girls hunched on enormous brown horses practically stepped over my little car as they passed. I watched as they kicked their mounts into a trot, onto the vast swathe of parkland I'd just driven through, then they just sparked into life. They rose in their stirrups, all flexing muscles and squeezing knees and toned thighs, leaned low over their horses' manes, stuck their tight jodhpur-clad bottoms in the air, and went from a standing start to full tilt gallop before you could say giddy-up.

There's something about the pounding of hooves, isn't there? It drums through your bones, even from a distance. Something exhilarating, and also threatening. I was breathing faster as I got out of the car and peered round for a kitchen door, a chimney, or a doorstep. A scruffy bloke in faded blue jeans and cowboy boots was forking up piles of dung and straw in the corner. I cleared my throat.

'Excuse me? Where's er – where's the house?'

He lifted his vast wheelbarrow, muscles twitching in his arms. Glanced briefly from under his long, messy hair at my bare legs and pencil skirt.

'What is this? A bloody Thomas Hardy novel?'

He shrugged, and walked away. I tried to get a look at him, but as I stepped forwards I slipped on the wet cobbles and turned my ankle, snapping my stiletto. When I looked up again, swearing, he'd disappeared. And it had started raining again. Hard.

That's when I nearly drove home again. No-one would be any the wiser. But that would have been stupid. The alternative on offer was an empty Saturday munching a take-away in Earl's Court.

I stomped grumpily into the nearest shelter while I decided what to do. Instantly my nostrils pricked with pleasure. The place was suffused with my favourite smell. Leather. The room was lined with gleaming saddles and bridles, shiny metallic buckles and snaffle bits, belts and harnesses and whips.

And in the darkest corner sat a huge Wild West style

saddle strapped to a kind of wooden bucking bronco. It was big and wide as an armchair. It had a huge, ornate pommel rearing up in front. That's for people like Clint Eastwood to idly rest their hands. I glanced out of the window. I was in the middle of nowhere. I looked back at the saddle. God, it looked so comfortable. I walked over the wooden floor, scuffing up sawdust, climbed aboard the wooden horse and swung my leg over the saddle. The flat leather seat felt warm as an animal.

I wriggled into place, hemmed in by the high back and the fat pommel as if I was about to ride into battle. Now I was astride it, my legs spread wide to get comfortable, my skirt stretched taught over the tops of my thighs, my knickers pressing on the wide seat. No wonder cowboys had bandy legs. If I pressed downwards, my pussy squashed against the leather, spreading the puffy lips open. Just flimsy pink silk separating them from the musky saddle. Think of all the bottoms, mostly male, that had straddled this seat. The soft balls hiding inside those button flies, the cocks resting there, safe from the chafing.

I moved slightly, and the headless bronco dipped forwards, tipped back, started rocking. A kind of grown-up's rocking horse! My legs were flopping about, feet dangling in the air, but I didn't want to stop. My cunt quivered faintly with the motion. The leather was heating up under me, as if I really was astride a sweaty mount, and it creaked as if speaking.

Outside, the wind rattled the stable doors and knocked over a bucket, but there was no one else here. Well, those lanky girls might come trotting back any minute. That oaf sweeping the yard was probably long gone. I glanced out of the window, imagined his dark, sardonic (or was that satanic?) face staring in at me, grasping his broom or whatever between big, dirty hands.

Christ. Anyone could come and stare in at me. What was I thinking of? That guy from the bar who invited me here, whose name I couldn't bloody remember, he could pitch up any minute looking for me. All his posh mates. The bloke with the mucky brush would have told him by now there was a townie bird tottering about the place in stupid shoes.

I jumped off my mount, heart pounding, blushing scarlet, pacing about as if I'd already been caught red-handed. Well, I'd just pretend I was someone else if he caught me. I don't know. The new stable hand or groom or whatever they're called. A rambler gone off track. He'd never know the difference. Cats all look the same in the dark, and we'd only seen each other, the other night, in the dark.

Anyway, the place was deserted. It was raining harder. The sky was black. My little car huddled by the crumbling archway. Any minute I'd make a dash for it. But first I wanted another ride in that saddle. It was stained dark deep in the seat, from all those sweaty buttocks rubbing and sliding. On impulse I peeled my skirt off, shoved my bare foot in the swinging stirrup. As I swung my leg over to climb back on, I felt my pussy parting. I'd heard of saddle sores. So I kept my knickers on, wriggled the pink silk down in to the saddle, smiling again at the creaking sound it made, like I wasn't alone.

I grasped the high rounded pommel at the front with one hand and the high, ornate back rest at the back and slid myself back and forth, smiling as the leather heated under me with the friction. Quickly my sex lips started to get sticky, vibrating with the heat. I speeded up.

'Giddy up, boy,' I whispered, wondering if I sounded like a nutcase. The saddle gripped the wooden bronco and the bronco rocked under me, using my rhythm but then its own momentum, getting faster, dipping its headless torso to the dusty floor, rearing and tossing me backwards in my seat.

All the while I gripped with my thighs, and the satin of my knickers slid easily across the leather. My knickers were getting really damp with the movement and my excitement.

The smell of the leather grew stronger, mingled with my own wet, sweet aroma.

I closed my eyes, raising myself off the seat as far as the long stirrups would allow me. They were extended, because cowboys ride with straight legs. Brits like those lanky girls shorten the stirrups, ride with bent legs. I pushed my knees into the side of the saddle and tilted my butt so that the chilly air could get to my pussy. Then I banged myself down on to the seat, rubbing frantically up and down the saddle, grinding myself against the skin surface so as to feel the heat in every crevice, spreading my legs wider so as to press my clit down and start rubbing some more. My thighs started to quiver, but I kept myself raised up and forward over the saddle, like those girls had done, allowing myself to be swung and rocked by my wooden horse.

The bronco got faster. It gave a kind of low humming as it rocked, as if it was breathing. My heart beat faster, too. There must be a switch somewhere. I didn't know then that if I stopped, it would stop. I grasped the high, rounded pommel to keep my balance, but as the bronco lurched forwards I fell against it. The thick, phallic stem pushed between my legs. It triggered a violent tremor through me and I gasped. I wanted something big and hard inside me. I clambered to my knees and lowered myself on to it. It was too big to get inside, but the shape of it was perfect for my private game, and before long I was squealing with growing pleasure as I gyrated round the thick leather stem.

'Did you know,' came a deep voice into the dusty silence, 'that pommel means 'little apple'?'

I groaned, nearly coming at the thought that someone else was there, watching me. I held myself very still, my butt in the air, my legs quivering with the effort of holding me in that position. Sure enough the bronco slowed down, but not entirely, so that I was forced to rock very slightly with it. My cunt was clenching ferociously with frustration. I could feel the juices seeping into my knickers.

'No,' I almost sobbed, twitching my hips slightly, arching my back. I held on to the pommel as if I was pole-dancing. 'But this little apple is about to come!'

There was a kind of snaking shiver in the air, and a loop of thin rope coiled round my wrists, wrapped several times round them, and lashed my hands tightly to the pommel.

The voice got deeper. 'And did you know that I don't take kindly to trespassers? Let alone little tarts writhing half naked on my pride and joy, getting it all wet and mucky. That saddle is worth a fortune. That's real silver on the buckles. Maybe I ought to get you on your knees, licking it clean –'

'I'll do whatever you like. Just don't stop me!' I wrenched at my restraints, but I was tied fast. I closed my eyes and sank forwards over the pommel. I was starting to tremble in the cold. 'And I'm not a trespasser. I was invited.'

'So who invited you? The lord of the manor?'

'Yes! Well, I *think* he's the lord – he didn't look particularly lord-like –' I tried to swivel round in my seat, but something hard and blunt prodded me in my spine, right between my shoulder blades, making me jerk upright. The rope bit into my skin like a vicious bracelet. I winced, but it was thrilling. 'Anyway, he'll tell you I'm his guest. I met him in London the other night. He asked me to come. I got lost, that's all. If you tell him Angela from Whispers Nightclub is here. The redhead. He'll know –'

'I'm not running your errands! Even if you are a randy redhead.' He was coming closer, his feet scraping across the floor.

'You're the stable-hand, aren't you?'

The rope jerked at my wrists from somewhere behind me. 'So what's his name? This best friend of yours who invited you down for a dirty weekend?'

I sank down into the saddle. The sound of my whimpering in the dusty silence turned me on. My skin was pricking up in goose-bumps. My nipples shrank back in the cold, poking against my flimsy shirt. I heard him smacking something impatiently in the palm of his hand. Smack, smack.

'I'm waiting for an answer.'

'I didn't get his name, OK? I could barely hear him speak with the noise and the music! He just gave me his address, and told me to come.'

'I doubt it. Angus would never just give his address to a complete stranger, however sexy. He's very private. So I'll do him a favour. Lean forward.'

I leaned forward, which made my butt jut instantly in the air. 'What favour? Who's Angus?'

There was a brief silence, then a swishing sound, soft as a whisper yet cutting the air. Then something whipped across my bottom, the sting instant and sharp. I gasped and flinched with shock.

'What the fuck!'

'Your punishment for trespassing.'

I bit my lip, humiliated by the pain. My butt cheek was smarting like fire. 'I told you. I was invited –'

'Not to swagger round my stables and straddle my best saddle, you weren't. Just stick your little bottom in the air. Higher!'

I pulled myself forwards, my fingers waggling pathetically. The rope manacles held me fast. But I liked how it looked. The helplessness. The hopeless tugging and pulling to get away. And I could imagine how I must look, bottom in the air, legs parted as I knelt on the saddle, flesh wobbling as he whipped me. Playing the pathetic little victim even though we both knew perfectly well that I was nothing of the kind. Not when these urges were twisting, uncoiling inside me. Not when I was enjoying it so much-

Now the sting of the smack was fading, leaving a surprising warmth spreading right through me. My cunt twitched, and tightened.

'I'm naughty, so naughty.' I heard myself whimper, though it sounded suspiciously like the gurgle of laughter. 'I'm sorry.'

He was up behind me now. I could feel his warmth, smell his sweat. 'Sorry? For what?'

He stroked the spot where the whip had come down, lightly with his fingertips as if tracing his own handprint. His voice was soft now, hissing almost. I arched my back like a cat, relaxed, offering myself to him.

'For being sad enough to drive through a wet weekend because some jerk gave me his number in a nightclub –'

The stroking stopped. 'Some jerk?'

I swayed my hips from side to side. My knickers were so damp now they were stuck up my crack, chafing at my sex, rubbing at my clit. The more I swayed, imagining him getting hard at the sight of it, the hornier I got.

'I mean, picking up strange women in nightclubs. Hasn't he got a woman of his own?'

'Plenty.' The stroking continued, so gentle I could barely feel it. The sting of the slap had gone. But I was tensing up now.

'Can I go now?'

The bronco and the saddle shook as he moved nearer. I turned, caught a glimpse of an arm in a shirt lifting, sleeve rolled up, and then there was a second slap, harder, on the same spot. The stinging went deeper this time, radiated further, on the already tender spot. I twitched and groaned again, unable to control my own reflexes. This was like being another person, in another body. A new body thrilling to the sexy raw pain slicing through me.

'You can go when the jerk has finished with you.'

He stroked my buttock again, harder this time, his fingers digging into the plump flesh, making me arch my back again as he slid the crop between my legs and up my crotch, hooking my knickers away so that they unpeeled and released the sharp tang of my excitement.

'Fuck,' he muttered. 'Any idea how horny a tied woman with a red, sore bottom and a wet pussy is? How about we go back to Whispers Nightclub, where they all know you, and show everyone what a dirty slapper you really are?'

'Let's do it. I don't care who sees.' I wriggled with pleasure at the thought of everyone watching me tied up like this. My wriggling earned me another sharp slap and as I jerked backwards I bumped into his warm, hard body. His strong arm snaked round my middle, squeezed the breath out of me, and slapped my other buttock, the one that wasn't sore. The shock was brief and breathtaking, the pain sharp, before the pleasure prodded once again at my ready cunt. I could feel it opening, twitching. I lowered my stomach, stuck my rump right up in the air and opened my legs. He smacked me again before the pain had the chance to fade. I strained back for more, really desperate to be smacked again, but now he was clambering up onto the saddle behind me. He knocked my feet out of the stirrups so he could put his own feet in, to get his balance, but that meant I had to use all the strength in my thighs to keep myself hovering above the saddle. I writhed against the hot, slippery leather, my wrists tugging uselessly at the rope, my knickers scraping at my clit.

I'd heard of people who liked to be smacked and always thought how daft. Men, mostly. Judges, politicians. I couldn't think what pleasure there could possibly be in prostrating oneself and begging to be punished, begging to say sorry, for some made-up crime, just to feed a fantasy?

And I'd never dreamed the pleasure, in being hurt and humiliated, could actually make you come.

Well, now I knew. How dark it was. And I wanted everyone to see me like this. Straining on the rope bound so tight round my wrists. Being helpless, out of control like this was liberating. Being a little scared, enduring a particular kind of stinging pain, was exhilarating. Being ordered about and struck and told what to do and what to

131

say and what to be, was a cheap, nasty thrill. And all the excitement wasn't even in my mind, not really, the excitement was all right here, throbbing between my legs, opening wider, getting wetter, wanting my invisible master to take me.

He was behind me, parting my legs now with his hands. I rocked against him, the rope biting at my wrists, and there was no tenderness, no foreplay, just his smooth round knob, jabbing at me as I rocked back, hard and ready.

'The jerk wants to fuck you, Angela.'

The voice cut through my thoughts. 'Sending messages to the stable boy now is he?' I could hardly speak, I was so breathless, tilting, rocking, my wet knickers snagging against my clit, the rest of me rubbing and grinding against the leather saddle.

'There's no stable boy here, Angela.'

His cock was nudging into my bottom, through my cheeks. He took my hips and tilted me, tearing my knickers sideways, easing it into me, into my sex. My cunt felt like a little mouth, nibbling, eager to suck him in.

'So where is he?' I let him manhandle me, push his cock into me, helpless and tied up as I was.

'Oh, he's right here.'

'Bollocks,' I gasped. The moan of desire was already gathering in my throat, but still I wanted to taunt him. 'Man like that wouldn't be hung like –'

'A stallion? Oh, you better believe it.' The cock pushed at me, opening me more. The earth was shaking now, but it was the drumming of approaching hooves. I smiled to myself. Hallucinating in this cold, dusty stable. My whole body vibrated as I edged myself backwards onto the waiting cock. We both heard the soft wet pop as it penetrated. 'Ask any of the grateful wenches around here.'

I laughed sardonically, but it came out as a growl. 'Like those sulky wenches riding out earlier?'

I pushed myself hard against him so that the cock

slipped easily inside. It was rigid, hard, and hot. My body gripped it greedily.

'Especially them. And here they come now.'

Christ. Here they came, indeed. The drumming hooves across the distant parkland slowed, became a brisk clopping echoing under the archway, slowing across the cobbles. The sulky girls were talking loudly now, turned on by their ride. I struggled hard, with the ropes, but each yank and pull only shoved him tighter inside me.

'They'll be livid to see me fucking a fresh guest after the night we had,' the guy said, thrusting so hard that I fell forwards, the pommel knocking the breath out of my chest and making me wheeze. 'They thought this was an exclusive country weekend. Admit it. So did you!'

The crop was back, tickling against my face, running down my stomach, down to where my sex gaped to hold him as we fucked. 'You thought the jerk was desperate for a girl, didn't you?'

I nodded, remembering how he looked in the bar, through my drunken haze. Smart enough in his suit, but a little sad.

The horses were snorting, right outside the tack room. I could hear leather creaking, buckles jangling as they were loosened, the girls joking about being starving and needing a stiff drink. They were a few feet away.

'They'll be in to polish the tack and put it away. Well trained, you see.'

I could only grunt like an animal, his cock filling me, thrusting me across the saddle, my buttocks wobbling against his taut thighs. I watched the shapes of the girls and the horses moving about in the dark, the horses being led across the yard to their stables. Then the scuffing of riding boots, kicking through the straw, picking up the tack, coming nearer.

'Let's give them a show, Angela,' he whispered, fucking me harder and faster now, banging me across the saddle.

'My latest filthy mare!'

'Hey, Angus, when's dinner?' Their boots stopped dead. The saddles creaked in their arms. A low curse shot from one of them. I couldn't see them, but they were staring at me on the Wild West saddle, being fucked senseless.

His dirty words drove me on, gasping and grunting, my thighs locked tight around the saddle, every nerve screaming to keep me upright as he fucked me, rode me like a filthy mare, grinding up me and up me, until I felt his cock contract and with a final violent thrust he spurted his hot liquid into me.

'Don't you dare come! I'm not done!' I ground myself frantically down, tighter onto him.

'Ride him, girl!' one of the girls shouted, stepping closer. 'Go, girl!'

So I rode him, bucking like the bronco under me, hair flying, thighs burning with the strain, his cock pumping inside me, until I came, the girls circling round to urge me on, just like I was in a show.

They were twins. Blonde and blue-eyed, and not remotely livid. Grinning. Jodhpurs tight across their crotches, drawing my eyes to their straining seams. One of them winked, ran her tongue across her mouth, raised her own whip, and disappeared to crack it onto my lover's arse so he swore and cried out and jerked hard, right up me, and I came, shuddering and bucking over the saddle, pulling him down with me.

After the gasping there was dusty silence. One of the girls untied my wrists. The guy buttoned up his flies and tossed me my tight skirt. The girls watched intently as I drew it over my soaking knickers, picked up my broken shoes.

'Welcome to my stable, Angela!' the scruffy bloke said.

Under The Oak
by Penelope Friday

She is leaning against the thick trunk of the tree, her hair brilliantly red against its deep oak brown. The morning sun is shining, and a light breeze rustles the leaves above her. It smells of spring, of new life, of warmth.

Her eyes are on the gaps between the line of bushes, straining to catch the first glimpse of him. When she sees him, he is strolling casually – apparently aimlessly – towards her, hands thrust deep in his pockets, an arrogant tilt to his head.

'Well, James, what a coincidence meeting you here,' she throws at him, the slightest smile passing across her face as if blown by the wind.

'Oh yes?' His hands are either side of her head, and he is bending over her. 'You didn't expect to see me, of course…'

She raises an eyebrow.

'Why, no, sir.'

He grins, and shakes his head.

'You lie, Stevens, you lie. There is no truth in you.'

He kisses her hard and she responds; her arms encircling him, her body relaxing into his. She laughs at his evident hunger for her.

'Is my surname such a turn on for you? Perhaps I should use yours, Hellier. Who knows where it might lead?'

135

'Stevens, I do believe you're trying to seduce me.'

'Not much effort needed,' she retorts, standing on tiptoe to reach his mouth with her own.

Abruptly, he pushes her back against the tree, his hands closing on her neck. She can feel his strength, though he has only a light hold on her; knows that he is by far the more physically powerful. Suddenly the breeze has stopped and there is a stillness in the air, as if the world close around them has held its breath; yet not so far away, she can still hear the bustle of the everyday world, all-unknowing of what is taking place here. Her heart beats a little faster.

'Say that again?'

'Ooh, threats of violence, Jamie boy? I'm so scared,' she teases.

'You should be.'

He smiles the lopsided smile that had won her heart despite the warnings of her classmates and her own mind. Her school tie has somehow come loose in his hands, and he is stroking it through his palms with a soft, suggestive motion. Her eyes are shining with anticipation of what's to come, but she's still playing the game.

'That's my property, James. I'd like it back, please.'

He grabs her wrists in one hand, and his eyes glint in return.

'I'm going to give it back to you, Ella. Don't you worry.'

And he is tying her wrists together; and she is making motions of protest, but never enough that he could seriously believe that she wants to escape.

'I'll have you recall,' she says, as haughtily as a lady can when her hands are tied together with her own school tie, 'that I have a position to uphold in this school.'

'Oh, lots of positions,' agrees James suggestively.

She gives a soft sharp breath of outrage, and pushes him with her bound hands.

'I am head girl, I'll have you know.'

'Mm-hm.' A sparkle of mischief lights his eyes. 'What do you think the headmaster would say if he could see you now?'

'That's easy,' she grins. 'Hellier, stop assaulting the young lady or you'll be expelled from this school as quickly as you can say your own name.'

'And am I?'

'What?'

'Assaulting you.'

'Oh, I hope so,' she breathes. 'I hope so, Jamie.'

'Now that,' he murmurs, 'that sounds like a come-on, Stevens.'

'My surname again. For someone who's about to get as close to me as one person can get to another, you're very formal today.'

'Then take this as a formal warning, *Stevens*,' he returns. 'Any more of your insolence, and I'm going to show you exactly how I treat girls like you.'

'Threat or a promise?'

And he is kissing her again, kissing her not simply with a passion but also a fierceness that she is not used to in him. A fierceness that she likes. Oh yes, she likes. He has pushed her hands – still tied – above her head, and she is arching back against the tree, her body moulding itself to his. She is hot, and wet, and *wanting*; but he... he has not finished teasing her yet.

'Threat *and* a promise,' he corrects her. 'If you're so worried about your reputation, however, I could just... leave?'

And he moves back, just slightly out of her reach, and looks at her quizzically. She does not have red hair for nothing. She tosses it, and shrugs, raising her chin to look him in the eye.

'If you want.'

He shakes his head slowly.

'Oh no, Ella, that won't do. Are you trying to say that

you'd be quite happy for me to walk away right now?'

No, her throbbing body says. *No*.

'Believe me, James, I could find another guy if I wanted.'

'Yes. Yes, you could,' he agrees. 'But would they do this? Would they make you feel like this?'

He has taken her back into his arms, one leg thrust between hers. He is rocking her gently, and then less gently, on his leg, his muscular thigh sending tremors through her body. His mouth is on her neck, on her lips; his hands trailing through her hair. She is making small plaintive cries of need, of wanting; pressing closer, closer, as close as she can get. He draws back.

'Would they?' he demands.

'Yes, oh yes,' she whispers, but she is not thinking about his question; has not even heard it.

She raises bound hands to him and strokes the sides of his face with delicate fingers, and…

'Oh, Ella, you kill me,' he groans, kissing her again as his fingers undo the top button of her blouse, uncovering the smallest area of bare skin.

She is looking up at him with desire in her eyes, but a smile ghosts across her face.

'Then die…'

He has caught at the tie between her wrists, and is swinging her round, turning her so that she faces the tree, and the oak-smell of the tree is suddenly strong in her nostrils. With his other hand, he is undoing the belt at his waist; and she can hear the sound of the leather slipping from its moorings.

'You do know,' he says conversationally, 'that you will need to be punished for suggestions like that.'

He has pushed her so that she is leaning in against the tree, her cheek against its rough bark, her breasts pressing against the firm trunk, her hands above her head. His hand is now exploring her leg, his fingers running up her thigh beneath the short skirt that holds so much promise. A quiver runs through her as his hand strays further. What will he say when he finds…

'Miss Stevens!' He sounds amused. 'Nothing? Nothing underneath such a short skirt? And you seemed such a respectable girl!'

'I am,' she murmurs against the oak trunk. 'I am respectable.'

'Then explain this.' She feels his hands lifting her skirt so that it gathers up around her slim hips, leaving her palely exposed to the elements – and to James. 'I don't believe that you're respectable at all, Ella. Not at all. In fact, I believe that punishment is in order, don't you?'

He is running the leather belt gently across her rear, the smooth soft feel of it setting every nerve ending tingling.

'Punish me,' she begs, rubbing her face against the tree, arching her back.

'Or would it be more punishment *not* to?' he asks gently. The belt is removed from her skin, and she feels his hands reach up above her head, to where her own bound arms rest. He makes a movement with the belt. 'I could just… tie you up here, leave you for one of the other students – or teachers – to find. How would you explain that, Ella?'

'You wouldn't,' she whispers, turning her head to fix opaque green eyes on him.

'Wouldn't I?'

Her teeth nibble at her bottom lip.

'Please?'

He smiles slightly.

'Since you ask so nicely, Ella, how could I refuse? And you deserve it, don't you?'

'Oh yes…'

He strokes his palm across her naked bottom, savouring the pleasures of its rounded shape. And then, without warning, the leather belt slaps against her flesh, making her gasp.

'More,' she pants desperately.

'I make the rules, Ella, not you. You are not the head girl taking a prefects' meeting. You are mine here. You will get what I think you deserve.' Though the words sound cruel, James's voice holds promise and laughter. 'Isn't that right?'

'Yes, yes,' agrees Ella.

She would agree to anything. They both know it. They both love it.

And the belt is whipping through the air again, slapping her skin, leaving soft red marks that burn with a heat that melts Ella from the outside all the way in. And she is groaning and gasping and 'Oh, oh, *James,* oh!' until her cries are lost in incoherence, and he can tell just from the jerky, desperate movements that she wants him.

Then the whipping stops, and he kneels behind her, soothing her soreness with a soft, gentle tongue that wets and calms – and yet excites. His hands are on her hips, turning her so that his tongue can reach inside her, flicking to and fro until she squirms and squeals with pleasure, pressing herself against his mouth. He twists her back round to face him, and her hands are in his hair, her nails scratching across his scalp as she encourages him with every movement of her body, every sound that sighs through parted lips. His tongue presses harder, firmer, until she cannot help but pulse around him, her hands tightening their grip on his head as she comes shamelessly, with desperate, helpless abandon.

And he is on his feet again and holding her, whispering in her ear as the world settles around her. Once more she is aware of the sound of conversation in the distance, the quiet murmur of traffic as it passes on the road.

'Ah, Ella, what would the teachers think of you now? Do you think they'd believe you if you said you hadn't wanted it, seeing you now with the glow of satisfaction on your face? No, sweetheart, they would know you for the liar you are. They would know that all your 'good girl' appearance is just a façade. They would see, as I see, the wanton that lies beneath that cool exterior.'

She sighs, resting her head on his shoulder.

'Only for you, James,' she murmurs. 'Just for you.'

'That's my Ella,' he says approvingly, stroking her arms with firm but gentle fingers.

She lowers her head and sucks his fingers into the warm depths of her mouth, savouring the slight saltiness of them, pulling them deep inside, licking them with her tongue, and then rejecting them, only to suck them in again.

'Oh,' he whispers low, 'Oh, you tease, Ella. You tease. You know what I want now…'

She looks up through hooded eyes.

'How much do you want it, James? How much?'

'You'll give me anything I want, though, won't you?'

'Perhaps,' she smiles.

He kisses her again, hard.

'Won't you?'

'I might.' She relents. 'I will. But because I want to, because it pleases *me*, my James.'

She sinks to her knees in front of him, feeling the grass tickle her legs; her hands struggling in their bound state with the button on his trousers. The zip is easier, and then her mouth is closing around him as it had around his fingers, but this time… she knows her own power as she hears his sharply indrawn breath and feels how hard he already is inside her.

She is consumed by the salty taste, the silky feel, the damp musk smell of him; and it feels – almost – as good for her as it is for him. She revels in the control she has at this moment, so different from earlier… and yet, earlier – she loved relinquishing all her power to him, giving him everything and demanding nothing.

And he? Oh yes, she knows that he has his eyes on her every motion; he has eyes for no one but her, just as it has always been when they have been together. He lives her,

141

breathes her, wants her, loves her, with everything that is in him. She knows it, just as he knows the strength of her feelings for him.

His breathing is quick and laboured, as she uses her mouth on his erection, caressing it with her tongue as she had his fingers. She slows, teasing him; then pulls away for a second, her eyes meeting his.

'And what do you think the staff would say to you right now, my Jamie? Do they often catch you with a girl on her knees before you?'

'All the time,' he lies with deliberate coolness. 'You're one of a multitude, Stevens; don't think differently.'

'Considering where my mouth is, that's a foolish sort of comment,' she throws back, knowing it is a lie, her teeth closing in gentle threat around him.

But it is just a game, and she changes tack, sucking and loving him with her mouth and hands. And he is groaning now, his hands on her shoulders, steadying himself. She is laughing softly, even as her mouth continues its movement; and the sound vibrates through him. His grip on her tightens involuntarily, and spurring her on until he can control himself no longer.

'Yes, *there,*' he sighs, and he slumps against the tree, his eyes flicking closed for the first time.

And she pulls him down beside her, and they lie in the grass underneath the tree, cuddled together in a tangle of limbs and racing heart-beats. Her head is on his chest, his arms curled around her. The midday sun is sliding across the sky when they move, James unbinding Ella's hands and returning her tie to her, with a loving smile.

'Ella,' he says seriously, 'that was incredible.'

'Mm-hmm.' She smiles. 'What do you think they'd have said if we'd *really* done this at school?'

And they laugh as they walk towards their house, hand in hand.

Festival
by Cyanne

I drove into the showground with a familiar feeling of excitement. I've worked at music festivals since I was about sixteen, when my friends and I would sort out the recycling at Glastonbury in exchange for free entry. Many a happy afternoon was spent in the sun, unwashed, on no sleep, throwing junk at each other, giggling, not caring.

This year, I was putting my degree to good use and working as an assistant sound engineer. As my car bounced over the rutted grass, all around me marquees were going up, huge PA systems were being rolled out of vans, giant sculptures and flags were starting to appear. The smell of donuts, barbeques and black fug from the generators floated in waves, and the sun gleamed white over everything. The workers shouted to one another, ribbing and laughing, and I could hear at least four different stereos blasting.

It's always the same, everyone's excited, up for a weekend of working hard, partying 'til dawn, working some more, and leaving with a fat cheque at the end of it. The punters wouldn't start arriving 'til the following day but the workers camping area was already buzzing when I pulled up. Multi-coloured tents stood at crazy angles, way too close to each another, interspersed with scruffy cars, sagging clothes lines and smoking barbeques. I'd worked with loads of the crew before so I was greeted with a barrage of hoots and hugs and had a beer in my hand before I had even parked. It was going to be one of those weekends.

The next morning we were all up early, bleary eyed already, to attend the crew brief in the main marquee. The obligatory 'roadie' uniform of scruffy combats or jeans, faded black T-shirt and numerous gadgets dangling from the belt was de rigueur, and I was no exception. You don't get a lot of women in this job. I'm generally treated like one of the boys but I wouldn't do myself too many favours turning up with nail extensions and full make-up, not that that's really me anyway. It was pretty hot so I had my long blonde dreads piled up on top of my head in a tangly pony tail.

I clocked Sean straight away at the meeting. I'm normally immune to the blokes at work, but there was something about him I was attracted to. Maybe not even attracted to at first, I just found him compelling, interesting. It transpired he was managing the 'unsigned band' stage, and I have to admit I was pretty pleased to be assigned to working the same stage.

I don't know what it was about him. He didn't look that different to most of the other crew, except he didn't have the beer belly, the roll-up dangling from the corner of his mouth, or the hot dog in his hand. His posture seemed measured, almost military. I wondered if he had been a soldier at some point. He was quite a bit older than me, probably in his late thirties. Even with his shaved head and heavily tattooed arms, he seemed somehow cleaner than the other crew, most of whom already looked grubby and bedraggled after only one night of camping.

The real work was to start the next day, but that afternoon we had to get everything set up and tested so it was ready to go in the morning. The 'unsigned' tent was small and dark, with no bar inside. Sean gathered the shoddy team, cokes and cigarettes in hands, and ran over what we needed to finish that day. His accent was a subtle Southern-Irish, possibly diluted from living in England for a while. His voice was authoritative, but quiet, almost sad. I was certain he was looking at me frequently, but it was hard to decode his gaze. It was not one of definite lust, or even the Carry-On film lusty playfulness I often got from the guys, more of curiosity, quite the same as I was looking at him.

The stage was already built and the lighting crew were working on building up the frame around it on which to hang the lights. A stage looks so glamorous from the audience, but up there it is actually a lot of metal and wires and heavy equipment, very industrial.

Sean didn't talk a great deal, but we were all there to get the job done, and it seemed to get done fairly quickly. The stage was soon surrounded on three sides by a complicated truss built of trios of poles on which the huge lights hung. Black drapes hung straight from the roof and down the back of the stage, closing off the artists changing area and all the boxes and cases and junk which infested backstage. The rear corners of the stage had rickety-looking metal staircases for the artists, and, while most of the working mess had been cleared away, the carpet was still littered with the occasional roll of thick gaffer tape, and odd screws and wires.

Sound is a great passion of mine, and I like to get it right. Also, as this was my first gig as an engineer, I wanted to prove myself, so after everyone was starting to disperse for the night I was double-checking the settings on the monitor desk by the side of the stage. Sean came striding up the staircase nearest to me and straight past me without a word. He inspected the hardware on the stage, tugging on wires, pulling cable ties out of his back pocket and securing them tight. His muscular arms bulged as he worked and I blushed, quickly going back to my work. Taking a roll of the gaffer tape, Sean busied himself taping down the wires across the front of the stage, pulling out huge lengths at a time and cutting it neatly with his Stanley knife. I don't know why I was so transfixed by him, but I watched him work. The night was starting to close in now and the last little bits of sunlight were coming through the gaps in the marquee in weak, thin strips. The dim, yellowish working lights were glinting off the light frame, the microphone stands and the drum kit, all reflecting each other. There is something so spooky about a space which is intended to be bustling with people when it is almost deserted.

Sean glanced in my direction and I panicked as he caught me looking at him, but my stomach lurched in lust at the same time. He was very attractive, and his eye contact, however brief, hit me hard. I took a deep breath and tried to arrange my thoughts. Sleeping with your boss on the first night of your first gig is not the best way to make friends in this business, I reasoned.

I don't know how he managed to sneak up behind me without me realising but I felt his eyes burrowing into me. I carried on with what I was doing, half joining in his game, and half genuinely freaked out. It is rare to feel this kind of chemistry but there are some people who can turn me on just by being near me, and here was one. I hated myself for it, but my breathing was getting shallower. Even though the sun was almost gone and the chilly English summer night was setting in, my cheeks blazed and dampened.

He was pretty close behind me, I was sure of that, and he was breathing in time with me. I wanted him, bugger the consequences, this man would be the best fuck in the world. Flashes of him grabbing me up in his big arms, kissing me hard, of the amazing hard body that was no doubt under his clothes coursed through my head. I had tried to resist, but what the hell, I'm a slave to my hormones sometimes. I slowly started to turn around, sure his face would be right behind me, and the kiss would melt the tension that was tightening my stomach and wetting my knickers. His hands

146

were suddenly on my shoulders. He pushed me forward, not roughly, but firmly, over the sound desk, the various knobs and dials pressing into my ribs, my breasts and my face. I enjoyed being handled by such a strong man, but I desperately wanted to kiss him, wanted to see his face.

I wriggled up onto my elbows, lifting my face off the desk, and heard Sean tut, almost imperceptibly. My hearing heightened by the proximity of danger, albeit very welcome danger, I heard a rustle as he pulled something out of his pocket. He leaned over my back, face close to my neck, crotch pressing against my arse, then the cable tie was in front of my eyes, then round my wrists. A zip, and it was pulled tight, my tanned arms bisected by the stark white plastic, just nipping into the skin, my hands totally immobilised.

I was shocked, a little scared even, I hardly knew this man, but there's something so freeing about being bound. I relinquished responsibility for myself.

Sean seemed to move more urgently for a second, flurrying to undo the button on my shorts. I writhed in anticipation, sure he was going to take my clothes off and fuck me, right here, but he seemed to check himself, and resumed his slow deliberate movements. How frustrating. I tried to arch my back, sticking my arse out, inviting him, but he just pressed me flat with his hand. My shorts were unbuttoned and the cold air grazed my skin as they fell to the floor. A deft movement and my pants were round my ankles too. I felt slightly ridiculous as he kicked my feet to step out of my clothes, humiliated by being naked from the waist down. My thong tangled on the hooks of my big boots and he bent down to tear it away. I looked around, checking for anyone left in the marquee. I could hear a distant party going on, but there was no one around.

A small guttural noise escaped from Sean as he smoothed his hand over my arse. I was wet. I was wet from his touch, wet from the tied hands, and wet from being so exposed and humiliated. His fingers squelched as they pressed into me and I cried out. Completely filled, yet still craving his kiss, his face in my hands, his hands on my tits. I fought futilely against the bonds. I was frustrated but his touch was expert, and I was building into a climax. How obscene I felt, my hands inextricably tied, T-shirt and boots still on, bent forward with my legs apart, naked arse and pussy presented up to this man twice my age, my clothes in a heap on the floor. The image tipped me over the edge and I came, arms and chest painfully pressed into the desk, gushing all over his hand.

I knew he'd be dying to fuck me after that. Maybe he would untie me and hold me in his arms and fuck me face to face, or maybe he'd leave me like this and do me from behind.

He dropped the small Stanley knife close to my hands, before walking away down the steps. I was furious, suddenly more embarrassed than before. I sawed through the plastic tie in a panic and pulled my lower clothes back on. I was horrified with myself. All kinds of thoughts started going wild in my head – how could I work with him now? What if he told people? What if he'd filmed what he did? What if he was back at the camp when I got back?

He was nowhere to be seen as I arrived back at the tents and I was thankful to drink whisky round the fire with the others, who all seemed to suspect nothing.

I had no choice really but to brazen it out the next day. Luckily the health and safety inspectors had turned up late and Sean was busy showing them round, then as soon as the day's bands started I was busy up on the stage. The following evening we had problems with the generators and Sean was caught up sorting them out. At the end of the gig, he was nowhere to be seen.

It wasn't 'til the last band of the following evening was playing out that I felt his eyes on me again. I was tired from partying the night before and didn't feel up to a mental battle, so I'm really not sure why I contrived to be the last person left at the end of the night. The next day everything would be over and the stage would be demolished, packed away into vans, leaving nothing but flattened grass and hangovers. Everyone on the crew was of the opinion that drinking tonight and working in the morning would be the best plan, but I kidded myself that I would like to get away early tomorrow and should pack away some of the sound equipment tonight.

The stage was a wreck. Fourteen different bands had graced it over the weekend and everything was in disarray with sticky beer spillages and forgotten T-shirts.

The sun was gone and the eerie light reminded me of the other night. I was sure Sean was close, and I kept telling myself that I wasn't interested but, of course, I wouldn't be able to help it if he forced me. The two sides of my brain bantered with each other as I set about wheeling some of the huge speakers towards the back stairs.

Sean strode up the stairs in his measured manner and I started to babble about how I was moving the stacks now before everyone was busy trying to work at the same time tomorrow. He just looked at me. He wanted me. My reserve disintegrated in the face of his strength. I've never met anyone I've responded to so totally before, and I couldn't let it go. Tonight, though, I wanted it to be on my terms. Our eye contact had gone on far too long for it not to be sexual, and I took the reins.

I hopped up on one of the big carpeted speakers and peeled my top off. Normally for work I'd wear an old sports bra, but that day I'd gone for a cuter, blue mesh bra which was a bit see through. I put myself right in his face, thinking if I didn't have him I would explode. The speaker was on wheels and, looking me right in the eyes, he pushed the whole thing backwards, with me on it, up against the lighting scaffolding at the back of the stage. He pulled a

149

loop of thick black wire down under my chin, hooking me to the metal triangle by my neck. Even though we had shared something the previous night, I still didn't know what he was capable of. The intensity of his gaze made me think he was, well, maybe not safe exactly, but that he wouldn't badly hurt me, so I made no move to extricate myself.

The cold metal was raw against my bare back. I wanted to hurry things along a bit, I'd been waiting all weekend for this. I wanted his cock, his mouth. He hadn't even kissed me yet. I reached behind me and unclipped my bra. He leaned in so close to me, his mouth millimetres from mine, so I could feel the heat of his breath, could smell him so deeply, feel the slight bristle of his chin against mine. I closed my eyes and my stomach leapt in anticipation of his kiss but all I felt was him roughly pull each side of my bra straps out of my hands and fasten them up again around one of the metal bars of the scaffolding.

I was starting to like the game, but it was him I wanted. I was tied by my neck and my chest, still half dressed. I dreamed of him slipping my trousers and knickers down and fucking me on top of the speaker, kissing me deeply and fucking me hard. I clawed up inside his T-shirt, feeling his hard chest, so manly, so strong; I wanted him to open up to me, to lose control inside me. I was getting wet being so close to him. I didn't want to wait any more. I started to move my hands down lower but he pushed them away roughly, grabbing both wrists, tutting and shaking his head. A tiny pang of fear again, a frisson, I couldn't get into his head, much as I tried. I wanted him to melt, to crave me, to succumb to the signals I was sending him and wetly devour me. But he wouldn't, he was so cold, nothing in his eyes but a vague amusement.

He got behind me, behind the metal triangle, and I felt more rubbery wire twisting and tangling around my contorted arms. I struggled a little bit, but only half of me

150

really wanted to get free. From the neck down I was bonded. A wire around my neck, my bra clipping me to the pole, my hands and arms twisted tight in a wire behind my back. The wire whipped past my face as he swung it around, wrapping my waist and chest before knotting it behind my back.

Sean walked a few steps away and admired his work, much the same as when he is balancing out the stage lights or listening carefully to the sound mix, head cocked to one side, considering if he could do a better job.

He strolled up to me, unhurried, pulled down the cups of my bra and took my breasts in both hands. The relief of a sexual touch, finally, rushed through my body, my pussy ached and I arched against the bonds towards him, my nipples burning under his hands. I sighed, closing my eyes, signalling for him to carry on. He either didn't speak the language of normal sexual signals, or he chose to ignore it. Most men would have carried on giving me pleasure, done more to make me lose control, want to have me moaning and writhing in their arms, hoping they would get similar pleasure from me, but he dropped my breasts, leaving me bereft. 'Please…' And there was that look in his eyes, and I did fear him just a little bit. He shook his head again, tutted, and started scanning the floor of the stage. The dusty carpet was littered with drumsticks, bottles, screws and tools. What was he going to do to me? I was craving him so much I just wanted him to do *something,* but what if he hurt me? He picked up a roll of thick gaffer tape and tore off the tiniest thin strip, a centimetre or less wide, nipped my lips together and stuck it diagonally across my mouth. I could still talk through the sides of my mouth, but it was distorted. I tried. 'Sean…' His eyes were stone cold and he shook his head. Another strip came off, and another, and he criss-crossed them over the sides of my mouth like cartoon stitches.

I wriggled against the bonds on my neck, chest and

151

arms, playing with the feeling of having my lips taped crudely together, imagining how much the sight must be getting to him, how soon he wouldn't be able to help himself. I played into his hands, starting to kick my legs around, and he played right back. Smiling now, in spite of himself, he got me out of my trousers, as I mumbled against the tape on my lips, pretending it wasn't the thing I wanted more than anything. Again, my boots stayed on. There is something more exposed about being partly naked, my bra roughly pulled down, my pants half down from the roughness of him pulling my trousers off, and my work boots still on. Being totally naked seems natural, being like that seemed so much more wrong. Waves of humiliation and pain, as the wires started to numb my arms, piqued my pleasure at having his undivided attention.

Another wire appeared and Sean had regained his composure, the glimmer of a smile gone. He looped the bright pink wire round one of my legs, slowly leading it round the back of the pole, and round the other leg at the knee, ending behind me with both ends. Gradually he pulled. The wires tautened, pulling my legs open. He stopped, and started, and stopped and started, pulling just past the point of discomfort before tying the wire at the back. I braced. The different bonds were working against each other now and it was uncomfortable. Every time I moved to take the strain off one part of my body it pulled another part.

Sean walked in front of me, looking intently. I was as tied as I could manage, my breathing was slightly restricted, my legs hurt and my mouth was dry but my skin was going crazy for his touch. Pulling out his Stanley knife he carefully snipped the sides of my pants, and they fell away like nothing. And he smiled, really smiled this time, and lit a cigarette. I had never seen him smoke before but I do know that when someone is smoking they tend not to do anything else for a couple of minutes. I craved him so much

I was going mad. I implored him with my eyes, moving in my bonds as much as I could to tempt him.

He walked away from me. I could see he was hard through his jeans, but he walked away. I could hear shuffling backstage behind the curtain as he moved boxes around. I was so aware that someone could come into the marquee at any moment, but I was totally stuck, unable to get free if I wanted to. I wanted him to come back. My muscles seemed to hurt more when he was gone, and I was more scared of getting caught alone like this than with him. I was dripping wet and swollen in anticipation and I wriggled on top of the rough carpet of the speaker trying to satiate myself, different desires and emotions conflicting in me.

It seemed like days, but was probably only minutes, 'til he came back. I was hot, red in the face, frustrated, and totally at his mercy.

His fingers were welcome, but I wanted more, and begged through my taped mouth. His mouth on my nipples sent lightening through me, my head starting to spin and my eyes streamed. He bent down over me, pressing his lips to my pussy finally. I was dying to dig my nails in and pull him closer to me, but was stuck with the tiny amount of contact he deigned to give me, only touching my clit with the tip of his tongue. My frustration tipped and I came hard. I tried to scream and the tape checked me. My hips bucked and the wires tightened, the wheels of the speakers clanking off the wooden floor. He pressed two fingers inside me and flicked his knuckles against each other, sucking my clit into his mouth, and I came again, shuddering wildly, all control gone.

Sean untied the sound system wires and left me alone, exhausted, to sort myself out of the tangle of tape and clothes.

The next morning I left early, driving back over the rutted field now littered with cans and paper cups. A general air of hangover presided. The night before had left me shell shocked. I had never been so completely satisfied by a man, yet still left craving him so much. We never even kissed, yet it was one of the most intense experiences of my life. I wondered about Sean, his past, his life, his motivations. I hadn't even begun to figure him out, but he had renewed my contract to work again next year, so maybe I'd find out then.

I dug around in the glove box for my sunglasses, protecting my sleep deprived eyes from the early morning sun, and pulled onto the motorway.

Mistress Of All She Surveys
by Carmel Lockyer

Valerie was waiting for a visitor. He was likely to be discreet, obsessively tidy and grateful. She had found him through the BDSM network, he was a Japanese devotee of shibari who had been transferred to a factory in Britain for a year or more.

It was all so easy, as neat as the symmetrical knots that her new client would desire to have tied in intricate profusion around his body. Beside her on the seat were a white rope and a red cord. She stretched out her left leg, admiring her patent leather Jimmy Choo boots and then ran the white rope through her fingers. It was twisted hemp, a traditional material for shibari, and it was her welcome gift to her new tenant.

Swiftly she roped her leg as though preparing for Aosagi leg suspension, finishing with a simple bight restraint. The binding was tight enough to make the blood surge and pump, loose enough to remain in place for several hours without causing her flesh to necrose. She was good at this. She was good at all of it: bondage, dominance, ritual humiliation and spontaneous pain. She could beat, bind, smack, provoke, restrain, inflict, subdue, ignore, frustrate and browbeat. But that was only half the story. People thought BDSM was an unequal process where one person got paid to hurt another, but from the inside the experience was intense, symmetrical, intimate. Doer and done-to shared richly textured pockets of time, where miracles were achieved by strenuous effort and complete trust.

She began to untie the rope, coiling it neatly into her hand as she worked.

It had been a labour of love, her apprenticeship. From the first time, at the first party, when she'd walked past the playroom and heard the unlikely rhythm of grunt, slap, gasp, sigh, she'd been hooked. Phil, the man she was 'seeing' then, had tugged her on towards the corner of the main room that was rich with resin and the pinched inhalation of huddled pot smokers. But she'd lagged, and – sensing her interest, still in the proprietorial phase of his lust – he'd wrapped an arm around her waist and steered her through the darkened doorway. As her eyes adjusted to the light – a red cloth swaddling the shade, she made out the scene as a kind of cameo. A roseate glowing, pearl-edged portrait of mutual need, being met in semi-public view.

The man was face down, bent over the end of a bed; his body much elevated by pillows and folded beds. The compressed fabric lay under his naked body like strata; layers of soft support. His arms were outstretched, palms flat to the mattress, like a deep obeisance, silver bracelets on his wrists, but the object of his worship was behind him. The woman stood with relaxed posture, her upraised hand Gnostic in its immobility. The prone figure's shoulders were high-hunched, his back ribs heaving gently. Pale except for his buttocks; they were rosier than a sunset. The first sense she could make of the image was that he resembled a rasher of bacon on its edge, pale and pink, thin and fragile. There was no detail to the woman, she was a dark form. Beyond her, shadowed and shadowy, a small audience clustered near the head of the bed. Phil tried to turn her round, but she locked her knees and his arm slid away as he half-turned back to the bonfire lure of Red Leb.

The pale figure lifted his right hand slightly from the

bed, just as far as the metal restraint allowed, and the woman swung her raised arm back, up, down. At the point of impact she grunted. The blow was deep, a resolute thwack, rather than a slap. The recipient gasped as the audience sighed. The smacked one lowered his arm, the woman raised hers and silence held the room until, after a few seconds, he lifted his hand again...

Valerie left the room, following Phil's energetic trek to mental wastage. She stood with him as he shouldered joshingly into the circle. But as he took his toke, holding the acrid smoke in his lungs with nonchalant ease, she slipped away, easing across the thin-carpeted floor heel and toe, heel and toe so as not to make any noise that could disturb the pot smokers.

The room had been brighter on her return – the cloth removed from the lamp. The woman stood, arms folded. She seemed de-animated, like a statue. In the cluster of audience, which she saw now was entirely male, the man with the roseate buttocks was being assisted in raising his jeans over his coral buttocks. Valerie couldn't conceal her disappointment; it scuffed her feet and pouted out her lower lip. Now, this Valerie looked back on that one with mild amusement. She had been only seventeen after all.

The other woman raised an eyebrow. She was nothing special to look at, but she held the room's energy contained within her. The huddle of men paused – rosy-bum even halted the zipping of his fly. They followed the woman's gaze, to Valerie.

That was the moment her love affair began. She could pinpoint it with the exactitude of a user's first fix, or a lover's first kiss. She had known then – without testing the knowledge against experience – that she could give so much more than the woman who stood before her. She'd gathered the eyes, assessing each man, reading their fluctuating levels of desire and fear, until she found the one who was most needy. She smiled at him, before looking back at the other woman.

The choreography of the group played out before her like a minuet. Two men refolded the bedding to make an altar for the chosen victim. Another took his clothes as he undressed. Valerie was pleased to observe his gently bobbing phallus. The chorus grouped around the bed, one of them checking the chosen victim's comfort as he stretched belly down on the heap of bedding, another laying the red cloth over the lamp with ceremonial exactitude, a third fastening the manacles around his wrists, trapping him against the bars of the bed-head.

The woman moved back to her place at the end of the bed, between her victim's parted legs. She quirked her eyebrow again, a mannerism Valerie would soon steal, along with the other's clientele. The chorus regrouped, huddling at the bed head, and Valerie stepped forward, to share the other woman's view.

The room settled into a tense expectation. The wait for something to happen was prickly, a hot feeling of restrained energy. Valerie realized, with a sudden shock, that the power in the room had shifted entirely – the woman was not in control. As soon as the prone figure gave its assent then she would be again the controlling influence in the room, but until then she was a cipher. It was the victim, the chosen one, the man who would submit to her blows, who held the power. The realisation went deeper still, to challenge what Valerie had thought she knew about the world – if the man had the power but suffered the pain, then who was really in control? Who chose? For decades she would explore that conundrum, testing the paradox of dominance and submission, pain and pleasure, against her own understanding until she knew all the turns in the path that two people could take when one had agreed to suffer and the other to impose suffering.

Then, in the moments that she waited for the man to abdicate his power and hand it back to his tormentor, she felt a vertigo better than sex. There, in that pause, she couldn't get her breath, heat spread from her sex down to her knees, up to the hollow of her throat, into the palms of her hands, so they tingled. The thready beat of her pulse banged against her skin as though crying to be let out. All these were stronger than sex, more exciting than the fairground rides she'd taken as a kid, richer than the effects of the dope that Phil made her smoke. This was it.

He raised his bound hand. The woman beside her swayed into the backswing of the blow, Valerie felt as though the air around her own body was throbbing with desire. The slap landed, the woman grunted, the victim hissed, the audience sighed. Valerie fell into the deep red space in her own heart that had never been troubled before. She had to be that woman. She had to do what the other was doing. And she had to do it soon, before the absolute lust for it destroyed her.

After half dozen smacks the other woman moved to the side, curling a finger to bring Valerie to take her place. The tension in the room rose palpably. Now, Valerie knew, there were a dozen places in the world you could share that collective moment: an opera house before a tricky aria; a bullfight in the seconds before the *toro* was released; an operating theatre before the first incision; a courtroom before the verdict was returned. She had tried them all, played with all the sensations available to her, but still that moment that first strike, was the culmination of her self. It was what had made her whole.

She had raised her arm, feeling her shoulder rotate out and back as though in tennis. She had waited for the signal from the figure on the bed, and then she had brought down her arm, hand open, neither tense nor limp but slightly cupped, flexed around a curve of air as palpable to her as a baby bird. Her hand connected with the flesh below her, compressing it against the bone beneath its domed surface. She felt her own bones, the phalanges of her fingers, spreading out from the impact, acted upon by the inertia of the form she had struck. It was delicious.

She couldn't hear anything now – if she grunted she was unaware, if the audience sighed she didn't know it. All she knew was the reddening pattern of finger-marks on white flesh.

It was only when the other woman took her arm and pulled her gently to one side that she realised the man had ceased to raise his arm. She would have waited all night for another signal from him.

And that was another paradox. Who was really making the choice and who abdicating? Did she choose to hit him, or did he choose to be hit by her? Had she picked him out, or had he chosen her? What was the contract that had been made in the few seconds she had spent picking out the man she wanted? Had she even known what she wanted, or rather had he known what he wanted and – in possession of that knowledge – imposed his need on her? Was she servant or victim, and of his needs or her own?

She had never found out. But the journey had been enough. It was like tightrope-walking with a balance bar of ice over a pit of flaming knives. The puzzles never ended. The best dominatrix was the one who'd trained as a submissive. The domme was the boss… although if the sub left they were still a sub, but the domme was nothing – her entire life was determined by the sub she dominated. BDSM games had rules as complicated and formal as chess, and yet the moment that everybody sought was the transcendent one when the rules fell away and sub and domme moved into headspace where there was no understanding of top and bottom, give and take, doer and done to, just the rapture of shared experience. Empathy and pain. Control and dissolution. Desire and repression.

The buzzer sounded. In the empty flat it had a strange ferocity. She stood and laid the rope gently back into the black velvet pouch she had bought to contain it. She lifted the red silk cord and tied it into a Turk's Head knot around the pouch. Only then did she stand and press the button that allowed her visitor to enter the building. Nakamura would be waiting patiently. It was in his nature.

She waited. There had always been a moment of dislocation when she met a new submissive. There would have been a period of courtship, through mutual acquaintances, while they learned about each other, his needs, her fees and so on. Both parties would examine the others past relationships to see what flaws or accidents had broken the bond between domme and sub. When they finally came face to face in a carefully orchestrated first meeting, she had always needed to adjust her mental picture to fit the physicality of the man who would be taller or louder or more or less attractive than she had imagined.

Twice she had been unable to accept the new client. The reality had been too alien for her to commit to the intimacy expected of her. The first man she'd rejected she'd heard no more about, but the second had gone on to become a real nuisance, a self-dramatist whose proclivity for dramatic self-harm and long name-filled suicide notes caused much trouble in the small BDSM community.

So, as she waited for Nakamura to climb the stairs, she emptied her mind of expectation. He was quiet on his feet she noted, for there was no clatter on the stairs. She knew approximately how long it would take the man to reach the top floor and at the moment when she anticipated his arrival on the half-landing she heard his step.

The knock on the door was moth light. Before she opened it, she rested both her hands for a second on the heavy wood.

Nakamura was slim and excessively deferential. She'd researched him carefully and she knew his tentative social timidity concealed ruthless business prowess. Most people thought that sexual submissiveness was a determining personal characteristic but Valerie's experience suggested there was no link between bedroom and boardroom. Some of her most extreme clients, who wanted to be 24/7 slaves, were powerful and decisive men in their offices.

He bowed low and Valerie inclined her head. They straightened and he bowed again, proffering a package with both hands. Valerie took it, hesitated for a second, and decided to open it. Normally she wouldn't open a client's gift in their presence. It heightened their expectation – would they be rewarded on their next visit or would an inadequate present result in drudgery without gratification, for which they would still pay handsomely? If she was disappointed by a client's generosity she made them brush the rugs with a toothbrush, or clean and polish her instruments of repression, before sending them home.

But Nakamura was not an ordinary client. His gift was not an attempt to win her favour – it was a courtesy. Inside the hand-painted paper was an ivory netsuke. That occasioned another pause. It was a gift out of proportion to the event. If genuine, and she felt sure it was, it carried a freight of expectation that made her uncomfortable.

She shook her head slowly, watching Nakamura in her peripheral vision. His face set in an impassive expression but his posture gave him away; the hunched shoulders of a supplicant and the taut, whitened knuckles of a man struggling to conceal disappointment.

She turned the figurine in her hands, admiring the lively detail of the carved monkey, watching the cool blue of the walls strike glacial highlights from the creamy surfaces.

'I cannot accept this gift,' she said. Nakamura dropped his gaze, shamed by her refusal.

'However…' she let the pause lengthen, watching a muscle in his jaw as it tensed and relaxed. 'I could try to earn it.'

His eyes widened and shock pulled his mouth open. This was the language of submission. Valerie smiled at his confusion, delighted by the effect she'd created. It was a

162

technique she'd used hundreds of times on her own clients to subvert their expectations and lower their resistance. A moment of role-reversal did more than hours of pain – it flattened thresholds, carving new channels for experience and understanding.

'Let me see…' she rubbed her thumb over the head of the netsuke. The apparently absent-minded gesture drew Nakamura's eyes to her hands, making him concentrate on the flexibility and power of her grip. This focus would further disconcert him. She was blending business with obsession and she felt warm. Moving people like Nakamura to where she wanted them, making them do as she wished but allowing them to believe it was their choice gave her a rush that was better than drugs and more lasting than sex.

She turned and set the little figurine on the bare windowsill. The north light bounced over it like icy fingers. 'I will set myself a task. To introduce you to three women who may make your time here more… demanding. If one of the three agrees to take you on, and you are able to serve her, I will keep the gift. If none of them does I shall leave it here.' She watched him in the window glass as he calculated swiftly what this would cost him. In effect she'd removed his power of choice: if he wasn't accepted by one of her three suggestions he'd find it hard to be taken by a top-class domme, but with her acting as matchmaker he would have to buy twice as many presents and pay higher introduction fees than he would have done on his own. She watched herself too, knowing that her long dark hair bound up in an intricate knot, her severe Armani suit and the crisp white shirt underneath with cufflinks like drops of blood, would all be carrying messages of arousal, pain and control to his subconscious. The tall boots with their shiny black surfaces and spike heels would be driving him into a passion – he would want to feel those boots digging into his spine. The longer she waited, the more intense his feelings would become – denying him any suffering today would make his suffering ten times as intense at their next meeting. This was why she was at the top of her profession – because she knew how to deliver pain.

She turned, smiling dazzlingly, and scooped up her package from the chaise. He bowed again as he accepted it, and then hissed in appreciation at the quality of the knots. When he'd untied the pouch, looping the cord over his hand with loving precision, he hissed again at the rope inside.

'I am honoured by your attention.' His English was superb, as she would have expected from a man who'd studied economics at Cambridge. 'And more honoured, to be part of your task. I am sure any person selected by you will exceed my expectations.'

Valerie nodded. Once again she had a client where she wanted them – in the palm of her hand.

Teaching Derek
by Primula Bond

Christ, we're bored.

It's not supposed to rain in Devon. There's a limit to how much decorating you can do to spruce up your idyllic country cottage for renting, before you're yearning for the doorbell or the phone to ring. But the job has to be done, and fast, otherwise our investment will have been wasted. In the absence of glittering visitors from London to entertain us, and also any sensible overalls, Jane and I have taken to dressing each day in ludicrous, inappropriate fairy-tale clothes, just to make each other laugh.

Today I'm Mother Hubbard, wearing nothing but a flowery pinny. Jane is Goldilocks in a see-through baby-doll. We've tarted up nearly every room except the sitting room, which is full of paint pots, brushes and fabric swatches.

Just as we're finishing our ham doorstep sandwiches and apple crumble, there's a rapping on the front door. We both drop our spoons in surprise. Jane is up first, smoothing the silk negligee down and flicking her yellow hair. A flush of excitement mounts her cheeks. I follow close behind her. Perhaps at long last those rough tough locals have sniffed us out. It's been bloody weeks since either of us had a man.

'Oh no, you don't,' I growl, pushing past my mate. 'It's my turn. You shocked the postman yesterday.'

I dash through the sitting room, the pinafore flapping between my legs. My back is cold.

'Sally Seaman? You called us last week. About the feature? We're from *Cute Cottages*. But we seem to have come at a very bad time –'

A tense-looking peroxide blonde in a tight pink suit is on the doorstep, accompanied by a spindly young man in a striped jumper and clutching a camera. They are both staring openly at me, half-naked, and Janie, totally see-through. We're both shivering as the wind nips past our visitors to get inside the warm house.

'Sal?' Jane glares at me. I shrug carelessly. 'What's this about a feature?'

'Yeah, I forgot to tell you. But think about it. It'll be brilliant publicity.'

'And company. At last.' A slow smile stretches across Jane's face. 'We've been starved, haven't we?'

I nod, grinning. We turn back to face our visitors.

'Come in, come in,' we chorus, throwing the door open wide. 'Now is a very *good* time.'

We prod the prim, unsuspecting magazine writer off the doorstep, and nudge the callow photographer, leading him into the cottage.

'There's so much to show you,' says Jane, lifting her arms so the baby-doll rides right over her tanned thighs. She's wearing no knickers. 'We think we've made it contemporary, yet enticing. We want people flocking here to unwind, you know? Relax.'

The boy is bright red, pushing his dark hair off his face with long fingers and staring straight at Jane's big red nipples poking through the flimsy material. She looks gorgeous. A wet dream on a wet day. I can see a bulge stretching his smart trousers. My stomach tightens.

'This is the main sitting room, which of course we will be stripping to its bare essentials,' Jane chatters, gesticulating about the room. She pushes the two of them

166

onto the sofa, right on top of the little damp patch where I was lying this morning, watching telly and masturbating with one of the paintbrushes, using the soft bristles to fire me up, stroking them across my tender sex, tickling my clit, then using the long, blunt handle to push up me, take the place of a real, live, throbbing cock. Oh, yes. Not even my sweet Jane knows about that… yet.

But for now I'm standing meekly beside her while she twitters and twirls and absently re-ties the apron strings so that a big bow now covers my bottom.

'Coffee?' I suggest, turning to walk into the kitchen and displaying my naked backside.

'As you can see, Sal's very domesticated,' laughs Jane, stroking my bottom as I pass her. 'We're a good pair, actually. I'm the creative designer, she's the dog's body.'

'I heard that!' I cough in protest and come back with two mugs of coffee. Jane drapes her arm across the mantelpiece, cocking her leg so that we can all see the red slice of her bare cunt.

'Think I look like an art deco figurine?' she asks, tilting her chin in profile.

'More like a naff shepherdess you could buy in Woollies,' I mock, reaching to tug her negligee down over her legs and deliberately brushing against her waxed snatch. She flinches and squeals, batting at my hand. I know it's with pleasure, not embarrassment, but our guests won't know that. The tip of her tongue pokes between her teeth. I come closer, put my hand on her hair, make as if to kiss her, then she tips her head towards our audience as if we're forgetting.

'Great coffee,' croaks the photographer. The lady editor slowly crosses one plump thigh over the other with a swish of stocking and a flash of lace camisole and flips her notebook to a blank page. The photographer hasn't even taken off his lens cap. He's huddled next to her on the sofa, clutching his mug between his bony knees and rocking

167

slightly.

'Light the fire, would you Sal?' Jane asks, smiling over my head at the visitors.

'Of course, darling.' I bend over the hearth like a parlour maid, fiddling with the kindling and displaying the shadow of my slightly parted bottom like it's some kind of jungle mating ritual.

'Lovely real fire, even in summer,' remarks Jane, stroking her toe lazily up my leg. 'It makes you want to just lie down on this rug, get some big hunky bloke to fuck you right here in front of the flames, you know? Especially when the weather is so shitty. We never close the curtains. No need for that kind of privacy, out here in the country. Open house, you see, for all gentleman callers.'

I laugh quietly, get down on my knees now. 'We live in hope.'

The lady clears her throat.

'So, if you love the cottage so much, why do you want to change it?'

'Well, it needs updating to a proper love shack, doesn't it? That's what tenants expect these days. Somewhere they can come for a really dirty weekend. And the décor when we bought it was, well, more chintz than chutzpah, know what I mean?'

'Sure.' The lady is writing something down, crossing her legs again.

'It'll make a sexy love nest for someone,' I pipe up, lighting the fire then sitting back to smooth my hands over my breasts, down over my hips, leaving sooty stripes all over my pinny. The photographer gulps his hot coffee down too fast.

'Yes. So what we really want to create is a place where really hot people will want to come, you know, rut like goats all weekend in the soft beds, here on the rug, out under the cherry tree, down on the beach, then go back to work satisfied. Actually, from what we've heard, these

168

hoary locals are hung like donkeys, if only we could entice them over the threshold, know what I mean?'

'It's dull as hell without a man. That's another reason it doesn't really suit us girls.' I brush at the soot marks, making my breasts jump and bounce over the bib front. Absently I rub at my hidden nipples, biting my lip with pleasure at the sharp response. 'I mean, Jane and I love each other like crazy and girl on girl action is hot, especially on a rainy afternoon, but you know, a red blooded woman needs a good hard cock occasionally, not just her best mate's tongue and tits –'

'That's exactly it. A good hard cock.' Jane echoes thoughtfully, swinging her leg about so that her slit visibly opens and closes like a little mouth. She cocks her head as if the idea is occurring to her for the first time. 'That's all we need, to make this place complete.' She allows a pause. 'Not shocking you, are we?'

Our guests shake their heads, hard, as if they're trying to empty them. We both focus on the young photographer. Actually he has beautiful green eyes, spaced far apart, and jutting cheek bones like Rudolf Nureyev.

'Good. So all we're saying is, we need some fresh meat. Young, and tender,' I muse, running my hands over the swelling tops of my breasts, pushing them together. 'God, that would be good.'

'You're cute, aren't you?' Janie suddenly walks over to the boy, sits on the arm of the sofa, letting the negligee fall away from her pussy. 'What's your name?'

'Derek,' he croaks, licking his lips.

'Time to get out your Hasselblad, don't you think, Derek?'

The lady nods quickly, lifting her head to examine the old beams. I reach under the pinny, flipping it aside to scratch at my fanny and giving a little moan of pleasure as I do so. Jane keeps her face straight. The lady editor nibbles her biro and uncrosses her legs again, glancing from Jane to

Derek, who's gawping like a rabbit in headlights.

'I'm sure you want to get to work,' Jane says, catching the lady's eye.

'Perhaps a guided tour?' The lady totters to her feet and holds the notebook in front of her like a shield. She titters. 'Of your love shack?'

'Absolutely Miss, er –'

'Shona Shaw.'

'Brilliant idea, Shona Shaw,' beams Jane. 'Ready, Derek?'

But Derek is looking past her, drooling across the room at me. I've flipped the pinafore right over to one side so that my pink slit is fully visible. Unlike Jane I have kept a neat line of hair curling over the crack. Two fingers separate the soft lips, and the pink flesh glistens as my other hand tiptoes up my thigh. Honestly, our guests are so shocked they can barely move, let alone protest.

I run my tongue over my mouth and moan again. My hand pauses as it reaches the first pubic curl, then I lift one finger and beckon to Derek. He sits up straight as if he's been shot.

'You'll see we've completed the bedrooms and the bathroom. There's a lovely attic, you can see right over the little harbour –'

Jane winks at me and leads the lady out of the room. I watch the cute twitching of her pert butt, the cute wet promise of what's tucked in there for me later. Then I get up and come across to Derek. I stand in front of him and untie my pinafore, unhook it from over my head, hold it in front of me like a matador in front of a randy bull. His hair is very neatly combed into a side parting, and I ruffle it with my fingernails. He swipes one hand at me in an automatic tidying gesture, his sleeve far too short for his long arm, and quick as a flash I've grabbed his bony wrist and tied the apron strings round it.

'Got to stop you running away!' I breathe, grabbing his

other hand, tying them together like manacles above his head. Then I hook the string round the leg of the heavy table behind the sofa. Derek is now sprawled on the sofa in front of me, hands tied, legs spread.

Out in the hall Jane is chivvying the lady into a pair of oversize wellies and out into the sopping wet garden.

'More so that you can get a view of the cottage and its surroundings,' she says, pushing Shona Shaw outside to high-step over the overgrown grass and duck under the dripping branches. 'I don't intend to do any gardening. Do take your time out here. I'll just nip back inside, see what's–'

I see her watching me in the doorway, arms folded. The breeze from the front door shivers over me, naked as I am, hardening my nipples, pricking up my skin.

'Want to taste a horny older woman, Derek?' Keeping my eyes on my Janie, I kneel up on the sofa, straddling my captive, pushing my pussy into his face. Jane walks to the table above his head, leans over it, her juicy tits dangling down. I press nearer to her, Derek helpless under me, feel his quick hot breath on my cunt, the jut of his nose against my clit, and I push harder, burying his face in my sex as I strain for Jane's mouth.

He starts to lick, what else can he do, his eager tongue sliding up my crack, and Jane kisses me, opening her mouth to suck at my lips and my tongue, Derek knocking me slightly with the urgent force of his lapping, and I lift myself very slightly away from him, push myself back, feel his tongue stretching to get at me, sending thrills up my crack already.

Jane pulls away. 'Something going begging down here,' she breathes coarsely, pointing at Derek's trousers. 'A great big porker just ripe for the taking if you shimmy round and take a look.'

I grin, my lips wet with Jane's saliva. Shona Shaw passes the window. A burst of rain has started and her neat

171

coiffure is all messed up. She's pulling the collar of her jacket up, patting at her hair. She stops, right there in the rain, when she sees what we're doing to her assistant.

Janie climbs up on the table and leans right over, so that now I've pulled away her tits are dangling in Derek's face where my pussy was. She swings them back and forth in front of his mouth. I know what that's like. Those juicy nipples like raspberries, dangling just out of reach, so warm and hard when you get them between your teeth, the reward you get for pleasuring her. He's licking his lips, swallowing frantically, trying to reach the nipples she's offering him.

But it's his cock I want. I can suck her nipples, she can suck mine, any time. I take hold of his trousers and yank them down. Christ, he's huge, and totally hard. And all mine. Not going anywhere. The young ones are always the best. He jerks about, perhaps a little anxious, his cock flopping heavily against his stomach. The apron strings are biting into his lanky wrists, so I take pity and cup his balls for a moment, gasping with laughter as he flinches and groans with pleasure.

Jane is panting now, lowers her tits, squashes them into his face, and excitement shoots through me to see his wet mouth closing round one taut nipple and biting hard on it. I know how she likes that. I know how wet it makes her.

My pussy is twitching frantically, wet from his mouth and wet from excitement, and I can't hold back any longer. Jane isn't so bothered about being fucked, though she enjoys it when it happens. I'm the one who goes berserk without taking a good hard cock every once in a while. That's why she's letting me have Derek. She'll do anything for me...

But I want her, too. We've been cocooned in this cottage for so long, I'm used to fondling her to really turn me on. Derek's cock is so big that I can ease the swollen tip inside me and still be on a level with Jane's little face as she leans to press her tits into his mouth. So I can still kiss her as our

172

prisoner sucks at her, as his cock grows even bigger just for having me spinning on it. My knees are shaking with the effort of keeping myself above him, but kissing Jane is the cream on the cake for me, sucking on her tongue while I make a boy fuck me.

'Now, Derek,' I murmur, tongue tangled with hers, 'Where were we?'

I move very slightly, slipping him further inside. He thrusts eagerly, and I pull away teasingly. My toy. Jane squeezes her breasts together, brushes her nipples over his mouth while I relent and rock gently, up and down, easing slowly down until his cock fills me. I tickle his balls softly again and he groans, muffled by the twin mound of Jane's breasts.

'What a thing to tell your mates, honey,' I murmur, keeping above him, gripping him with my cunt, holding on to his shoulders, kissing my Jane. To keep him in place I have to do the work, keep moving and tilting, almost dancing up his length as I start to engulf him. My pussy lips nibble, just as my mouth is nibbling Jane's, and the excitement is overwhelming.

Once or twice his cock nearly slips out again, so I make tiny fast movements, plunging harder onto him, pulling Jane's head down so I can keep kissing her. He's groaning loudly now. Jane's nearly suffocating him. I'm working him like an instrument, mercilessly using him, all he can do is lie there, tied to our table, while I luxuriate in the knowledge that I could keep him there all day if I wanted to, my own sex toy. Our sex toy.

Friction sparks up me then dies, sparks up again. Doubt he's ever done this before, had two women writhing all over him. I bet he thinks he's died and gone to heaven. He's groaning and swearing, losing what little control he had, bucking furiously under me as Jane starts to moan as well. I wonder if she's fingering herself, but when I glance I see she's released one of his hands from my apron strings and is impaling herself on his free fingers. Christ, that's so dirty, using him like that, it makes me grind even more furiously, his cock right up me now, my hands squeezing her breasts too, pushing them into his mouth, soft and warm, my cunt gripping his cock and clenching –

And through the window, don't forget, Shona Shaw, watching the lot!

We all speed up, excitement mounting, his cock is rock hard inside me, and he's starting to come, I can tell, his cock is swelling and pumping, and I can't help it, I'm grinding down on him, faster, faster, lapping at Jane's mouth, knowing she's being fucked by his fingers, we're all in ecstasy, bands of excitement tightening inside me, and then he comes, I come, his spunk spurting up me, making me scream into Jane's face, hearing Derek's muffled yell as she stuffs her nipples further into his mouth and gives one of her sexy shuddering climactic moans.

I roll off him. Jane jumps quickly round to lie next to me on the sofa. Derek looks at us embracing each other. His mouth is drooling open. He stares at his wilting cock.

'Are you alright, Derek?' I ask him, twining my fingers in Jane's hair.

He flushes scarlet, yanks his hand out of the remaining tie, and scrambles to his feet, muttering to himself and hopping about trying to zip up his trousers.

Shona Shaw is in the doorway. 'Job done, Derek?'

'Oh, fuck,' mutters Derek, sidling towards her. We start shaking with silent laughter. There's frantic whispering at the door, and a creak of floorboards and the rubbery sound of discarded wellies.

'I should say that's a wrap, wouldn't you, Derek?' giggles Jane, and we're off in uncontrollable laughter. 'Got what you needed, Shona?'

Shona plucks at her assistant's sleeve. 'Everything I need,' she says, flushing. 'Now come along, Derek.'

Derek troops obediently after her, throwing a yearning

look over his woolly shoulder. I run my finger down my cunt, where he's just been, then lick it like a lollipop.

'I dare you. Give her one, Derek,' I call after him.

The door slams behind them, and we rush to the window. Shona is wagging her finger at Derek as he, aware that we're watching, attempts to accelerate the car manfully over the pot holes in our lane.

Jane climbs on top of me, rubs her sore nipples into my face. 'That's your man quota for today,' she growls, writhing against my pussy. 'I need some real loving now.'

I laugh, licking one cute nipple. 'She'll be so horny after watching all that, I bet she'll have Derek in a lay-by before they reach the M5!'

Political Prey
by Jim Baker

So this is it, the last night.

He looks so peaceful, sound asleep on the bed.

I'm tempted to keep him longer but I need to get away, take a break.

It will give me a disposal problem, but I managed the others.

Is it really only three weeks since I first saw him walking down the street?

I lifted the edge of the curtain and watched him. He was calling at all the houses in the street. He was carrying a clipboard in one hand, and a briefcase in the other. There was a big red rosette on his lapel. He looked young, although he was still too far away for me to get a good look at his face.

Young ones were always more fun.

I let the curtain drop, went through to the lounge, and poured myself a whisky and soda. I had plenty of time to get dressed. The black miniskirt and a tight silk blouse should have the desired effect, especially with the top three buttons of the blouse undone.

The bell rang about fifteen minutes later, and I opened

the door.

He gaped at me and almost dropped his clipboard.

Well, I may not have quite the figure I had when I was wrestling professionally, but I do look after myself. I work out at least three times a week in the gym.

I waited until his gaze had gone from my tits to my legs and back up again.

'Yes?'

His eyes met mine and I smiled at him over the rim of my whisky glass.

'Um, yes. Hello. I'm David Peterson. I'm canvassing for Simon Jones. Local politician. For the council. This is my official badge.' He waved a piece of plastic at me as the words tumbled out. 'I wondered if we can rely on your vote?'

'Well, I'm not sure. Why don't you come in and tell me more about Mr Jones?'

'Oh, well, yes, thanks.'

'Come on through. Sit down.'

He followed me, sat down on the settee, and stared around at the prints and drawings of the nude figures that adorned the walls.

I kicked off my shoes, sat down beside him, and let him extol the virtues of Simon Jones. He showed me figures to prove how much better off I'd be with Simon in power, opened his briefcase, and thrust leaflets into my hands. I let him talk while I examined him more closely.

I guessed him to be in his mid-twenties. He was thin, scruffy, and pasty-faced. There was the shadow of a beard on his chin and he needed a haircut. His fingernails were bitten to the quick and there were ink stains on his fingers.

But his hair was dark and curly and his eyes deep blue. I pictured him naked, spread-eagled on the bed…

I suddenly realised he had stopped talking. He was staring intently at me.

'So will you vote for Simon?' he asked anxiously.

'Of course.'

He looked relieved, took a pen from his pocket, and made a note on his clipboard.

I put my hand on his arm.

'You're very persuasive. Your wife must be a very lucky woman.'

He laughed, bitterly.

'I'm not married. Who'd want me?'

His face flushed and he started to get up.

'I'm sorry,' he said, embarrassed. 'I should finish the street.'

I increased the pressure on his arm.

'Don't be silly. Stay and talk some more. It's David, right? I'm Susie.'

He sank back wearily against the cushions.

'Thank you, I don't get to talk to many people. Especially to attractive women like you.'

'David, you're very kind. Would you like a drink?'

I persuaded him to take off his jacket and tie, brought him a whisky-soda, and let him talk.

It was a sorry tale.

He was twenty-five. He had dropped out from university after a year of studying history. His parents had left him enough money to buy a tiny apartment in a seedy area of town. He'd had a series of no-hope jobs that had earned him just enough money to eat – badly, I suspected.

'Like this canvassing job,' he said.

'What about friends, David?'

'No one, really. I go to the pub sometimes and talk to people.'

'Have you got a girlfriend?'

'No.'

He stood up, walked across the room, and studied one of the nude drawings.

'Do you like nude pictures, David?'

'No, I mean, yes…' he stammered. 'Did you do this?'

178

He reached up and touched the reclining nude form.

'No, David, that is me.'

He snatched his hand away and I laughed. 'It's all right, you can touch me if you want. Come back and sit down. Have another drink.'

I brought him a very strong whisky-soda, and he gulped down half of it.

His face was losing its pallor. I leaned forward to give him a really good look down my blouse, and stroked his cheek with one finger.

'Would you like to kiss me, David?'

'Oh, yes. Please.'

I put my hand behind his head and turned his face to mine. His lips were closed, and hard.

'Open your mouth a little.'

His lips relaxed. I heard him gasp as the tip of my tongue found his. I kissed him hard, sucked his tongue into my mouth and unbuttoned his shirt. He moaned as I pinched his nipples between my fingernails. I bit into his lower lip and sat back. His hands were trembling and his forehead was shining with sweat.

'David,' I whispered. 'Have you ever made love to a girl?'

He shook his head.

'Not really.'

'Tell me.'

He told me of a couple of pathetic attempts at college. His face burned red as he tried to find the words to describe his premature ejaculation, and the way that both the girls had laughed at him. Later on, he had tried with prostitutes, who had taken his money and sent him on his way.

I set my drink down, put a finger on his lips and pushed him back into the cushions.

'Stay still.'

I pulled his shirt from the waistband of his trousers and tossed it across the room. He was thin and his skin was virtually hairless. He quivered like a nervous puppy. I kissed his chest and licked his nipples then took his hand and used it to fondle my tits through the silk of my blouse.

'Take my blouse off, David.'

His hands shook as his clumsy fingers worked frantically at the tiny buttons. At last he succeeded, and pulled the blouse out from my skirt. He stopped, uncertain. I let it drop to the floor, reached behind me, and unhooked my bra. Leaning forward I put my hands on his shoulders and let the bra straps slide down my arms.

'Take it off, David.'

He pulled the bra away, and fixed his eyes on my tits.

I lifted them towards him.

'Feel them, baby.'

He cupped them in his hands and my nipples grew hard against his palms. I guided his head down and held him against me.

'Kiss them, David. Suck my nipples.'

I kept my hand on the back of his neck and closed my eyes, savouring the sensation of his clumsy efforts. My nipples tingled and I felt the familiar heat building between my legs. I raised his head from my tits and looked down at the bulge between his legs.

'Someone's getting pretty excited. I think we'd better let him out, don't you?'

I unfastened his trousers and pulled down the zip.

'Lift up, baby.' He raised his bottom, and I hooked my thumbs in the waistband and hauled them down to his thighs.

His cock was straining against a pair of white underpants, with the head just protruding from under the waistband.

I reached down and squeezed the shaft through the fabric, and ran the tip of my index finger up and down the little ridge of skin behind the head.

His body jerked as if he had received an electric shock

and the breath came out him in a long rattling gasp.

I rolled the pants down, and pulled them away.

Not all of him was thin and scrawny. A long, thick rigid pole of flesh sprang free.

'My, David,' I said, softly. 'You are a big lad. Those other girls don't know what they missed.'

I slid down on to my knees on the carpet and took his cock in my hand. Beads of clear liquid pre-come oozed from the slit.

I rubbed my thumb through the slippery liquid and spread it across the hot, bulbous head. His breathing was getting faster and it was clear he was close to coming. I wrapped my hand around the shaft and felt it swell.

'Come on, sweetheart,' I whispered. 'Come for me. All over my tits.'

I pressed the head into my cleavage and worked his foreskin up and down in a series of rapid strokes. He gave a great rasping groan. His cock jerked wildly in my hand and the first jet of hot fluid splattered between my tits. I gripped him tightly until his cock stopped pumping, and then squeezed out the last drops as he fell back, eyes closed, against the cushions.

I picked up my whisky and sipped it, relishing the warm feel of his sperm trickling down my body.

At last his eyes fluttered open and he looked at me, dazedly.

'Come on, lover-boy,' I said. 'We both need a shower.'

I stood and took his hand. He rose, clutching his trousers, and followed me on shaky legs down the stairs to the basement bedroom.

'The shower's through there. I'll be right back.'

He stripped and went into the en suite bathroom. I picked up his clothes, went out, and locked the bedroom door behind me.

I went up to my bedroom, stripped off my skirt and panties, took a hot shower and lay down on the bed, fantasising about what the next few hours would bring.

After about half an hour I prepared the drugs, and put the syringe on a tray. I slipped into a fresh pair of panties and went back downstairs.

I unlocked the door and looked inside.

The combination of whisky and sex had worked.

He was sound asleep on the bed, with a towel draped across his lower body.

It's always the best time – the first few hours, when they don't suspect anything.

You can let yourself go, and really have fun.

After that you have to be careful.

I slid the tray under the bed, sat down, and pulled the towel away.

His whole body was thin, almost emaciated.

His cock was lying on his stomach, soft and defenceless.

I stretched out on the bed beside him, took the flaccid flesh between my fingers, and played with it. I put my face close to his and watched as he woke.

'Hello,' I whispered.

His eyes widened and his cock grew in my hand.

I took his hand, guided it down between my legs, and rubbed his fingers up and down in the crotch of my panties.

'Feel how wet I am down there, David,' I whispered. I took his fingers under the waistband and into the hot damp forest between my thighs.

'That's right, David. Play with my pussy. Do you know where to touch a girl to drive her crazy?'

His cock grew like a steel rod and I stroked it slowly while I used my other hand to lead his finger to my clit.

'Gently baby – oh, that feels good!'

I let him play with me for a few moments, and then took his hand away.

'Would you like to take my panties off, David, and put

your big cock right up inside my hot cunt?'

'Please!' The word croaked from his throat.

I teased him for a while, and eventually let him take my panties off.

'Come on, darling,' I whispered, rolled on to my back and splayed my thighs apart.

I waited until he moved between my legs and then, as he rose over me, I lifted my legs around his waist, crossed my ankles behind his back and took him into a wrestling leg scissor hold.

Before he could begin struggling I rolled back on to my side and began to squeeze, tightening my thigh muscles across his stomach.

I wanted that cock inside me, but first I needed to find out how strong he was.

My experience in the world of female wrestling has left me able to handle almost anyone who isn't either a pro-wrestler, or a lot stronger than me.

It didn't take long. He struggled a bit and then groaned as I increased the pressure.

'Please…' he whispered.

I held him a little longer, then unlocked my ankles, turned him on to his back and straddled his chest.

I looked down at him.

'Right, David,' I said. 'You can fuck me. But first you're going to taste me.'

A bit of early domination is always a good idea. And having control over a guy always makes me incredibly horny.

I shifted up until my crotch was over his face, ground my knees into his biceps, and lowered myself until my pubic hair touched his chin.

'OK, baby, this is your first lesson.'

I settled my cunt on to his face.

I stayed there for a long time, making him suck and lick.

Three times I let my whole weight rest on his nose and mouth, grinding my cunt into him until he was desperate for breath.

At last the friction of his tongue on my clit made me shudder with pleasure, and I lifted myself off, rolled us over and pulled him down between my legs.

'OK, David. Fuck me.'

He was clumsy, and I had to help him, but I finally had his big cock inside me, stretching the flesh of my cunt, and he thrust like a madman. He came in about two minutes, long before I'd started to feel anything.

But he was young.

A short session with my fingers and lips and the pole of flesh stood upright again, ready for action. This time was slower, and I groaned with delight as the orgasm rippled through my body and I felt him spurting inside me.

After that I became a teacher. I showed him how to use his fingers and his tongue to give me pleasure, and let him explore my body while I played with his. He was like a kid in a sweetshop.

We fucked twice more. The final time, I got on top and rode him, and I came twice before he reached his orgasm.

Finally he fell into an exhausted sleep. I dragged my body off the bed, took the syringe from the tray, and gave him an injection.

I opened the cupboard and took out the steel chain and handcuff. I checked the wall fastening, made sure the chain had no tangles that would prevent him reaching the bathroom, and clipped the cuff to his wrist.

Then I staggered upstairs to another hot shower, more whisky, and my bed.

That was three weeks ago, and now it's our last night.
He looks so vulnerable, asleep on the bed with the chain

draped across him.

David was very upset when he realised he was a prisoner, but, like the others, he soon came around.

After he realised that yelling and screaming weren't going to help – the bedroom is soundproofed – he tried attacking me.

Sadly, I had to hurt him. It only happened twice. The second time I hurt him rather badly.

Since then he's been docile, and the drugs have kept him very, very horny. He has learned an awful lot about how to keep a woman happy.

It took me a while before I got the drug combination right, but there's a lot of information on the Internet.

Anyway, he deserves one last treat; I'll wake him up with a glass of champers and a nice slow blow-job. It'll be easy to give him his last injection just after he comes.

Maid To Misbehave
by Stephen Albrow

Madeleine glanced up and down the street before entering the sex shop, nervous of anyone she knew seeing her visiting such insalubrious premises; terrified, too, of what she would find behind the mysterious dark blue door. Her only other visit to a sex shop had been during a weekend trip to Amsterdam, where her husband had dragged her through a neon-lit doorway. That store had been full of dirty-looking men rifling through racks of hardcore magazines, but she sensed this one would be more her style. Not only was it labelled an erotic boutique, but also it sold some high-quality products, judging by the beautifully tailored French maid's outfit she'd spotted in the window.

She'd first seen the uniform three weeks earlier, but it had taken her all that time to pluck up the courage to enter the boutique. She passed the store on her way to and from work each day, but had never seen anyone come or go, all of which added to its sense of mystery and foreboding.

The windows were blacked out behind a colourful display of lingerie, so there was no way of knowing what it was like inside. Taking her courage in both hands, she entered.

Seated behind the counter was a dark-haired girl, with kohl-rimmed eyes and crimson lips. Her hair was pulled back away from her face and tied into a ponytail, which dangled down her back like the train of a whip. She was flicking through a magazine, and she didn't look up. Glad of this, Madeleine hurried to the nearest rack of lingerie.

The girl's presence was intimidating, although she couldn't quite put her finger on why.

Shielded by a row of corsets and basques, Madeleine took a furtive glance around the store. Most of the stock consisted of leatherwear, sex toys and erotic lingerie, rather than the hordes of magazines and XXX DVDs that were popular with the raincoat brigade. She felt relieved to be the only customer, but at the same time it unnerved her.

Her heartbeat drummed against her ribcage, as she tried to pinpoint the French maid's uniform, keen to buy it and get out of there as fast as she could.

She tried to move quietly but the laminate flooring was unforgiving. The click of her heels echoed loudly round the otherwise completely silent store.

The store assistant looked up from her magazine, frowning as though annoyed to be distracted from her reading. Like many shop assistants, she didn't ask if Madeleine needed any help. She just stared at the customer; her dark eyes widening, fixing Madeleine with a look of contempt.

For a second Madeleine thought about leaving, but she *had* to get what she'd gone there for.

She remembered how she'd felt the first time she'd spotted the outfit. It had unlocked something within her, giving body and soul to fantasies that had been floating vaguely around her head since she was 19 or 20. She'd always had a secret urge to wear that uniform, and to see what affect it would have on her husband. Sex between them had been boring of late, in fact almost non-existent. But maybe the outfit would trigger something – the sub-dom role-play she'd always craved.

I've wanted this for ages, she thought, worried it might be her last chance to change things. It wasn't easy bringing up the subject of bondage eight years into a marriage, but the new uniform would be a talking point, so perhaps it was the answer.

Ignoring the shop girl's disgruntled expression, Madeleine approached the counter. She felt the flush of a newfound determination, but it vanished when the shop girl rose from her chair.

Madeline stared. The girl was six feet tall in her stockinged feet, only she wasn't in her stockinged feet – she was wearing thigh-high boots with six-inch heels.

Madeleine, who had come straight from the office in her kitten heels looked up open-mouthed. But it wasn't just her height that was overwhelming. Her legs were endless and her torso voluptuous, with full breasts and graceful hips. Her tight, clingy rubber mini-dress had a daringly plunging neckline. It was shrink-wrapped to her, tighter than a corset, emphasising her hourglass shape.

'Yes?' said the shop girl, rather than asking if she could be of help.

'I'd like to try on the French maid's outfit.'

'Really?'

'Yes, really.'

'We can sort that out,' she said.

She stepped from behind the counter and walked to the window.

Madeleine watched, determined not to run. Her stomach churned nervously as she worried about exactly what she was getting herself into.

The shop girl was suddenly all action, hurrying back with the outfit.

'Get changed in there.' She pointed to a curtained cubicle in the corner of the store. The way she said it made it sound like an order, but Madeleine didn't mind being bossed about, since it helped remove any doubt from her mind. Just as seeing the French maid's outfit in the window seemed to have unlocked her latent submissiveness, so something about this tall, beautiful, rubber-clad shop girl was doing just the same.

Happy to obey, Madeleine entered the cubicle, drew the curtain and then took off her work clothes. There was a mirror on the nearside wall, so she held the uniform against her body, smiling as the soft, silky fabric touched her skin. She put on the lacy head-dress first, then was about to step into the short, black frock when she heard signs of movement in the boutique. The shop girl's heels click-clacked on the floor; was that a key being turned in a lock?

After a moment's pause, the footsteps resumed, moving steadily in the direction of the changing room. The curtain was yanked back.

The girl was carrying a pair of frilly panties, two hold up stockings and a pair of high-heels.

'You will wear these.' She dumped the items onto the changing room floor.

'I've got a pair of tights on already.'

'You *will* wear *these*!'

The girl drew the curtain back across, then commanded Madeleine to hurry up. The matter wasn't up for discussion. Madeleine would wear what she was ordered to wear. And she wanted to.

Bewildered but carried away by the other-worldliness of it all, she removed her tights and knickers. It was a curious moment, because, as she took her knickers off, she realised how moist she was.

Experiencing excitement and concern in equal measure, she pulled on the satin panties. The fancy frills made her bum look extra curvy, and were sure to look incredibly sexy when she bent over in her tiny maid's dress. She eased the stockings on next, the sensuous fabric caressing her upper thighs, then finally it was time to don the outfit of her dreams. Such a perfect fit! The tight bodice top helped to push up her generous cleavage, while the saucy pleated skirt, complete with lace-trimmed apron, fell an inch below

189

her stocking tops.

After slipping her feet into the high-heel shoes, she caught sight of her reflection. The uniform offered her the chance to become a totally different person for an hour or two. She hoped her husband would see the change in her, but first she'd find out what the shop girl thought.

She drew back the curtain and posed. 'How do I look?' She bent over so the dress rode up and flashed the girl her stocking tops and panties.

'You look like a slut,' the girl replied, her gaze transfixed by the maid's frilly panties. She spoke jokily at first, but then her eyes seemed to harden. 'And sluts deserve to be punished,' she yelled, her chilling manner sending an icy shiver down Madeleine's spine.

The girl stepped behind the counter and fetched the chair on which she'd been sitting. She commanded her to lie across it. Madeline glanced across at the door. The 'Open' sign had been turned to 'Closed.'

'But you made me wear the slutty panties and stockings,' argued Madeleine, suddenly feeling out of her depth.

Her heartbeat doubled, her stomach churned and her body now felt extremely vulnerable. The skimpy uniform left much of her flesh exposed, not least the highly spankable zone between her stocking tops and panties.

'Lie across the chair, you slut,' screamed the girl, walking to a nearby shelf. The boutique was a dominatrix's paradise, since there were restraints and punishment tools dotted everywhere. The girl picked up a length of cord and a long rubber baton. She waved it through the air.

Stirred into action, Madeleine lay across the chair, her bottom poking up in the air. The girl knelt down beside her, then used the length of cord to tie the French maid's body to the wooden chair. She pulled the cord tight, then made six more loops, only stopping once Madeline was securely trussed up. Even her arms were bound up with her torso, rendering her absolutely helpless.

As the girl stood up, Madeleine wriggled, testing to see if there was any give in the cord.

The six-foot-tall girl stood in front of her, her legs slightly apart, allowing Madeleine to look up her rubber mini-dress. She wore no knickers and her sex lips were glistening.

'Only sluts like French maid outfits,' said the girl, her lips curled into a malicious sneer. She started circling Madeleine's body, the dagger-like heels of her thigh-boots beating a menacing tattoo on the laminate floor.

Madeleine knew she was going to be beaten with the baton, but the girl seemed determined to keep her waiting, knowing the delay would set her already frazzled nerves even further on edge. The ominous sense of foreboding was almost too much for the captive maid to bear, so she raised her buttocks a little higher, as if imploring the girl to get the punishment started.

'Such an eager little slut,' said the shop girl, as she delivered the blow that Madeleine craved. The rubber baton struck the mid-point between her stocking tops and panties, sending a twinge of pain through her sensitive flesh. She had often dreamed of role-play, and had always assumed it to be a playful thing, but the girl's opening strike made it clear that this punishment was being played out for real. The second blow was no less certain, the thwack of the baton against Madeleine's thigh causing a fractured howl to burst from her lips.

'Silence, slut!'

The baton was raised again. She trained a blow on Madeleine's buttocks, but it was cushioned by the lacy panties. The shop girl pulled them down.

With her cheeks uncovered, the shop girl dealt out blow after blow.

Madeleine imagined the bright red marks all over her behind. She howled, and would have writhed in agony were her body not bound so tight by the cord. The girl was taking her right to the brink with the unrelenting force of the beating, but for all the agonising, torturous pain, something positive was happening – a rich, warm glow was building in her sex.

'You really are a slut,' said the girl as she swung her arm forward. As the rigid rubber shaft met her soft, smooth buttocks, Madeleine threw back her head and roared. But this time it wasn't a howl of pain – this time it was a cry of pleasure! Being bound and beaten by the gorgeous young shop girl was fulfilling her inner urges like never before.

The beating was painful, but Madeleine knew she needed it, just as she'd known she had to wear the French maid's uniform. Something very deep inside was being brought closer to the surface with each new blow from the rubber baton.

It was hard to admit, even to herself, but she loved the way she was being dominated; loved being treated like a sexual toy; loved being punished for the worthless slut she knew she was. The shop girl was young, tall, beautiful and domineering, which made her superior in every way.

'I am unworthy of you, Mistress,' Madeleine said, the admission like music to the shop girl's ears. She was about to deliver a further strike, but now she stood before the maid, instead. She hitched her dress up and pressed her sex into Madeleine's face.

'Prove to me you can be worthy,' said the girl.

Madeleine knew what was required. She began to kiss her pussy. She tasted the juices on the girl's pink lips, saw the pink velvet flesh rich with fluid.

Madeleine licked and sucked, her feathery touch making the shop girl groan. 'Good slut,' said the girl, leaning over Madeleine's trussed-up torso, the baton gripped within her hand. Madeleine steeled herself for a burst of pain, but the rubber length didn't strike her arse – it pressed between her cunt lips instead. She gasped, as its hardness entered her, but quickly regained composure, her lips surrounding the shop girl's slit. The girl was pumping the baton back and forth; Madeleine returned the compliment. She tongue-fucked the shop girl's sticky cunt in perfect rhythm with the baton's thrusts.

A fierce wave of tension flooded Madeleine's pussy, as the rigid length powered to and fro. Her insides spasmed round the rubber shaft, which was sparking tingles of pleasure over eight-inches deep inside her body. She felt grateful to have a mistress who was willing to grant her these moments of joy, and was determined to pay her back in full. So she stuck out her tongue as far as she could, reaching deep inside the shop girl's cunt, then she licked with passion, forcefully, devotedly, till she felt the sticky juice shower her face.

As the rapid tongue-thrusts brought the shop girl to a climax, so the baton began to pick up speed. It plunged deep between Madeleine's gaping lips, waking up every nerve ending inside her hole, and the extra sensation was enough to send her spiralling into a blissful orgasm. Her pussy muscles contracted hard, then the excess tension made her scream, but not for long, because she was too keen to lick up more of the shop girl's luscious cream. A sticky spray of come wet her cheeks and chin, as her tongue re-entered the girl's pulsing gash. Then the baton came to a halt inside her, as the girl threw her head back and screamed.

Madeleine watched, as a jolt of electric tension coursed through the shop girl's body. She clasped her breasts, pumping her pussy back and forth, making her lips slid all over Madeleine's face.

The girl was overwhelmed with pleasure, and Madeleine felt just the same, but her body couldn't twist and writhe like hers, thanks to the cord that bound her to the chair.

This final sign of the shop girl's dominance added further fuel to Madeleine's orgasmic fire. Her submissive immobility, her sweet surrender, made her pussy muscles pulse and thump; made a torrent of sex-juice rush through her tunnel. The baton was still pressed deep between her cunt lips, and closing her eyes, she imagined it to be her husband's tumescent cock. If her maid's uniform could stir in him the same kind of dominant passion it had stirred in the shop girl, then their love life had a chance to blossom again. He could be master to his lowly slave.

'I'll take the uniform,' Madeleine said, her body still aglow with climactic joy.

'And the panties, heels and stockings?'

'Yes, everything,' said Madeleine. 'The cord, as well. And the rubber baton.' She wanted to be able to recreate everything exactly as it had been. That way she could relive and recapture the same incredible orgasmic high

The shop girl smiled. She had managed to make her sale, but she didn't go rushing to the cash register. She kept her smooth shaved lips pressed tight to Madeleine's face.

'More,' she said.

Madeleine knew what she meant.

Eager to serve, and to keep on exploring the submissive side of her nature, she kissed the shop girl's pussy. It was dripping wet, which delighted her since it was proof of the shop girl's intense satisfaction.

The French maid's outfit felt right on her. No, more than that, it *belonged* on her, as the shop girl had been quick to notice. Now, hopefully, her husband would be equally intuitive, and by seeing Madeleine in the uniform, he would pick up on her deep-seated need to serve and obey. If so, it was a chance for them to start afresh, an opportunity to experiment with something new. Oh, the fun they would have, as the powerful master dished out orders to his pretty maid! Oh, the greater fun when she failed to complete them and had to be punished for her errant ways!

195

Also available from Xcite Books:
(www.xcitebooks.com)

Sex & Seduction	**1905170785**	**price £7.99**
Sex & Satisfaction	**1905170777**	**price £7.99**
Sex & Submission	**1905170793**	**price £7.99**

5 Minute Fantasies 1	**1905170610**	**price £7.99**
5 Minute Fantasies 2	**190517070X**	**price £7.99**
5 Minute Fantasies 3	**1905170718**	**price £7.99**

Whip Me	**1905170920**	**price £7.99**
Spank Me	**1905170939**	**price £7.99**
Tie Me Up	**1905170947**	**price £7.99**

Ultimate Sins	**1905170599**	**price £7.99**
Ultimate Sex	**1905170955**	**price £7.99**
Ultimate Submission	**1905170963**	**price £7.99**